UNVEILING
the
DARK SECRETS
of
SPIRITUAL WORLD

A True Life Depiction

ALEX NGUYEN

HUYNH MY TRINH

eBook ISBN: 978-1-965064-63-4
Paperback ISBN: 978-1-965064-64-1
Hardback ISBN: 978-1-965064-65-8

Dedication

To Readers,

For every reader who dares to embark on this journey with me, may these pages ignite your imagination and touch your soul. Your curiosity and thirst for knowledge are the fuel that drives authors like myself to keep writing. This book is dedicated to you, with heartfelt thanks for joining me on this adventure.

Acknowledgment

I would like to express my deepest gratitude to my wife for her unwavering support and encouragement throughout this process. Her strength and belief in me have kept me going through the difficult times.

About the Author

Alexander Nguyen received his Bachelor of Arts in Science in 1996 and graduated Summa Cum Laude. He has worked tirelessly to improve the lives of the less fortunate and downtrodden in both the Juvenile and Adult Justice Systems. He retired in September 2022.

Alexander is a retired Peace Officer in the State of California who worked 24 years in areas that included Domestic Violence, Gang Intervention, Drug Addiction and Recovery, Juvenile Drug Courts, and Family Violence Intervention.

Contents

Chapter One — The Inevitable

It was a rainy Saturday night, which was extremely usual for Northern Californian weather, especially in January! I mean, is it supposed to get colder now? I'm eagerly waiting for the sun. I'm completely done with the two-minute cold of Northern California. I had already freshened up and got into my pajamas since I was ready to continue our favorite TV show, which we always binge-watch every Saturday night. I made sure to order my wife's favorite takeout, which was Bangkok Express noodles, which I despise. I ordered double cheeseburgers and their loaded cheese fries from In- N-Out with extra pickles and onions for myself and our son, Brandon. Trina does not approve of our eating choices since the ol' man is forming a big belly. And quite frankly, I am developing a very distinct belly, which I need to lose ASAP.

I used to come home rather early since my shift ended at about 6 pm, and I had to wait for my wife, Trina, who worked at Bella Italia. That Italian restaurant was extremely popular in the area. Trina used to come home by 9:30. I, on the other hand, was a probation officer, and I had been a probation officer for the last 12 years. I mostly like my job, although it could definitely get a little challenging at times. It was a challenging and tiresome role, which might take a tremendous toll on an individual's mental health. Although I was almost toward the end of my career, I was 49 years old and was planning on retiring and leaving my probation officer career to the books.

The only thing that excited me at that time was my couch, and I looked forward to meeting my beautiful son, Brandon, at the end of every day. The main reason I was contemplating retiring was because that job provided me a great pension, a great deal of medical benefits, and a monthly stream of rental income from several residential properties I had given to rent all across California. Just so that I could provide whatever it was that my family might need in the future.

On the other hand, there was my beautiful wife, Trina, who I cannot envision a life without. I met Trina when I was just 22 years old, and the moment I met her, I just knew that she was going to be my wife. Trina made my life complete, and she brought the happiness and comfort that my heart eagerly yearned for every day. She made our home complete. I don't think any other woman would tolerate everything that Trina tolerated from me. She had been the type of woman who ultimately spoils whoever is dear to her rotten. Everywhere she went, she spread sunlight with her grace and beauty. At first, when I got to know her, I wasn't sure if her father would let us get married because he was extremely overprotective of her. Trina was the sort of person where family members and even extended family and friends would come and ask her to cook for them or ask for advice.

It was going to be a good Saturday night!

I switched on the TV box, and the first thing that popped up was the massive shipwreck that took place in Costa Concordia, where the 60,000-ton shipwreck took place, which was almost about to hit the Tuscan island of Giglio. I was in utter shock and disbelief, and I couldn't believe that such a monstrous ship could just simply capsize. I mean… that ship was twice the size of the Titanic, and for it to just collapse and start flooding was unbelievable. Who would've thought that luxury couldn't save lives? That ship had almost 3,000 passengers. I hoped they all made it out on time.

I checked the time, and the clock hit 10 pm; I was not sure where Trina was? Her shift usually ended by 9:30, and she should be home by now. As I roamed around our lounge, I cracked myself a can of beer to wait for my wife so we could have dinner and continue our favorite TV show. Our home, our humble abode, was a cute place that Trina and I liked to call our lodge. I remembered the first time we got it and how very excited we both were to decorate the home. It had been exactly two years since we moved into this home, and it screams *TRINA* all over it. As soon as you walk in, there is a large central hallway that meets with the wide wooden staircase that paves its way to the upper floor.

Trina made sure to incorporate her Vietnamese routes by hanging famous Nguyen Gia Tri and To Ngoc Van paintings in the entrance, with loads of just us. Us the best couple in the world. Toward the right of our home's entrance is our dinner table, which is made out of pure birch wood that Trina's father, Bruce, gifted to us when we got married. Adjacent to that is Trina's most cherished cupboard, which is a rare Vietnamese-inspired wooden cupboard that is engrossed with floral prints all over it. Trina loves to treasure antique pieces of cutlery, collects them, and stores them all in this cupboard. Right opposite the cupboard, there's a small pathway toward our lounge and kitchen. Our lounge is the coziest place in our house since we spent all our bucks on investing in the coziest couch.

You see, we both are couch potatoes, and we spend most of our time in the living room. Every time Trina and I have friends over, they always rave about the couch because it's the comfiest couch they've ever sat on. Our couch is a tufted chunk of cotton engrossed in a faux leather lining where you feel like you're sinking into a cloud that wants to grapple you in the instant you sit on top of it. Across from this dreamy sofa stands a pristine, sleek TV that is perfectly positioned for Trina and me to have an optimal view. Trina makes sure to have loads of comfy blankets kept right next to the couch because she has plenty of family and friends who love to use them when they are over. As one would make their way upstairs, we have two spacious bedrooms, one of which is the master bed, where Trina and I sleep. Then there is another room opposite ours, which is always open to family and friends since we have no family members in this house other than just us.

As soon as I turned around, I heard the doorbell, eagerly waiting for Trina's arrival. I paved myself through the living room toward the entrance when I realized that it was my burger that had just arrived! Haha, my bad. I guess old habits never die! My food had arrived, and Trina hadn't yet. Let me give her a call. Ugh, now I've got to locate my phone. I have just purchased an 'iPhone' box, and supposedly, that's the new innovation. I personally find it pretty complicated since I haven't gotten used to using a touch-screen phone like that. Although it was a gift from my wife this Christmas, I'm eternally grateful, not just for the gift but also for my wife, Trina.

The clock almost struck 10:30 when I heard the doorbell ring again, but this time, it rang twice, and in a distinct way, I knew it was Trina. My sweet wife has finally made it home, and I couldn't be happier.

"Hey, baby! What took so long?"

"Hi, ugh. Nothing, I was just at the gas station, picking up a few things that we needed. It started pouring out of nowhere! And I am soaked! How was your day?" Trina uttered.

"Meh. It was the same old!" Trina was soaked, with droplets of water running down her hair, visibly leaving a mark on our light brown wooden floor. I was just happy she was home. She handed me the plastic bags of groceries that she had brought from the gas station. I headed toward the kitchen, which is right ahead of our living room. Our kitchen was my safe haven. Trina made sure to always stock up the fridge with groceries and snacks so I wouldn't have to be hungry every time she wasn't home.

"Go, freshen up. I'll put out the food, and then we can continue Downton Abbey."

"Alrighty, baby!!"

As I put down the groceries on the dinner table, I noticed an envelope in the bag, and when I began to open the envelope, I noticed that they were a bunch of lottery tickets that Trina had purchased. If I'm being honest, I don't really believe in lottery tickets because I myself have wasted time purchasing them, and they're up to no good! I set the lottery tickets aside since I am aroused to see what came upon Trina to purchase these for the hundredth time!

Trina freshened up and came down to the dinner table, all ready to eat and start our TV show. As she proceeded to sit down and start eating her dinner, I asked, "Hey baby, how come you bought more lottery tickets? I thought we weren't going to buy those anymore."

"I'm not sure, actually. I just felt like buying the tickets because I was feeling lucky today," Trina said, looking up at me. Her eyes gleamed with hope and nervousness. And honestly, Alex, we're getting old. Might as well try to collect as many lottery tickets as we can. You and I both have seen so many people win these lotteries, so why can't we? Trina uttered.

"Yeah, I guess. Although I believe that they are a high-time scam and they just like taking our money. Anyways, how much did you buy 'em for?" I asked.

"I bought two for a dollar, then the other two for $10 and $20," Trina replied.

"Trina! We were supposed to save money! And you know how I feel about these lottery tickets."

Deep down, I wanted to believe Trina's optimistic and wishful thinking, although I had zero hope for these lottery tickets. They are just a waste of money and time. It's just a scam for working-class individuals to just hold onto hope and keep on hoping!

"Alex, don't remind me... You're the one that just bought a recreational vehicle, and now you're planning to troop over all the states and relax! So how am I wasting money?" Trina responded with the utmost sarcasm.

After we devoured our food, Trina cleaned up the kitchen table, and we proceeded to make our way toward the couch. This was our daily suit since we loved to watch our favorite TV show by the end of the day. I quickly picked up the lottery tickets and a pack of chips so we could munch on them together.

I sat on the couch without grabbing my glasses and laid my feet to rest on the coffee table opposite me. I reached into my pocket to get a nickel, to scratch the lottery ticket that Trina was so eager to foresee. I let out a large sigh and began to scratch the card when I saw that our favorite TV show, Downton Abbey, was about to begin.

"Hey Trina, get in here! The show's about to start!"

"Coming..."

I proceeded to scratch the lottery card when I noticed the letters 'A' 'N' 'O' began to appear. All of a sudden, I was extremely invested and anticipated what this lottery ticket might have in store for us. The metallic scrapes filled the surroundings of the paper as I slowly unveiled each other, and symbols glimmered with hope. Everything around me certainly stopped, and my eyes were just fixated on the impending moment of suspense. I was unable to comprehend what these first three letters meant.

"TRINA! Get in here, right this instant!" I yelled with frustration.

"Alex, SH! The neighbors will hear you! What is it?" Trina inquired. I could hear the tap running at the back, and Trina was just doing the dishes.

"No! You come here right now! It's about the lottery ticket!" My eyes were about to bulge out because I had a feeling that we were onto something.

Trina made her way to the couch with the red wine that she had placed on the coffee table. She seemed so confused and immediately came and sat right next to me. I passed her the lottery card and showed her what I had scratched up till now.

"Alex, you couldn't wait for me?"

"Trina!!! What does this mean? I am utterly taken aback! I want you to scratch the rest of the card because you're definitely the lucky charm here."

Trina proceeded to scratch the rest of the card while I was sitting back and praying to the Lord to have mercy and bring us the wealth! She scratched the following two lines, and unfortunately, there were no winning numbers or symbols that implied that we had won the lottery. I thought to myself, man, what a tragedy. Who are these people who actually win the lottery and are so lucky to be given that amount of money?

I leaned back toward the couch to watch our TV show while Trina wasn't giving up just yet. She continued to scratch the rest of the lottery card with a nickel, hoping that something might come out of this. Regrettably, no luck was found in Trina scratching the lottery card. Until she turned the card around and discovered this side had to be scratched out, too.

"You're wasting your breath, Trina. There's no point," I said while slurping my beer up.

She proceeded to scratch the back of the card when she discovered more letters that spelled out 'T' and 'H.'

"Hey, Alex, look! I'm definitely onto something here, and this is very unusual for a lottery ticket."

Trina and I were perplexed and unable to figure out what exactly this meant. I huddled over her, trying to get the best view of the card, and Trina scratched the numbers and symbols. I eagerly waited. A surge of excitement coursed through us as I thought to myself, we might have a second shot at fortune beckoning with the possibility of untold rewards. Trina continued to scratch the rest of the card, and the remaining letters were 'E,' 'R,' 'C,' 'H,' 'A,' 'N,' 'C,' and 'E.'

"Oh my gosh!" Trina blurted, a quiet laugh escaping in a sigh.

"Wha? What? What does that even mean?"

Trina and I both exchanged a glance of satisfaction and hope because we both felt extremely hopeful and lucky. This is extremely rare; we have purchased a thousand tickets in the past, and they never proved to be lucky. This time, when Trina randomly bought one from the gas station, it said that we had another chance.

"Let me google what this means, Alex," Trina said.

As she picked up her phone to check what this meant, I could see her eyes sparkle with joy and certainty.

"Alex! Basically, this means that for every past lottery ticket that we have purchased, we just have to draw them in, and one of them will certainly be a winner!"

When I heard Trina say that out loud, I was in disbelief. I couldn't believe what she was saying. I was unable to comprehend what was happening because this meant that we could be possible winners of the lottery in the future. I mean, how is one supposed to feel afterward? Trina is definitely my lucky charm, the only individual who brings me fortune and blessings in every chapter of my life. She brought my biggest blessing into this world: my son, Brandon. She's not merely a companion but a beacon of luck for me, a guiding star that has constantly been illuminating my path through life, through thick and thin. Trina's unwavering support and love have become my strength in this life. And I'm not just saying because we might have the possibility of winning the lottery, but I genuinely mean it.

For the past three years, Trina and I have constantly been collecting more lottery tickets and turning the previously purchased lottery tickets in, eagerly waiting for the day that the lottery winners will be announced. Don't get me wrong, it was a tough ride. Our patience was running thin, and there was constant chatter about what we would do once we won the lottery and what we would make sure not to do when we won it.

At times, it would feel like it's just a dream that we keep running after, and forth goes our dream. At times, I would feel stupid to turn over all our older lottery tickets because it seemed like such a waste of time. Our endless journey began with Trina and me gathering up lost lottery tickets from anywhere, and I entered the 19-digit code for each ticket. The hope that clung to our chests for the past three years has not been easy. The lottery winning had become our symbol of freedom, resilience, and a guiding light through our financial struggles and unforeseen challenges.

In October 2015, our lives changed forever. For better or for worse, I'm not exactly sure. I remember sitting on my couch and going about my day when I checked my inbox and got an email with the subject, 'An important message awaits you from the California Lottery.' I recall almost spitting out my coffee!! I remember going into a state of shock and excitement all at the same time. It was a whirlwind of emotions. The email then specified, *"You have won $10 Californian Lottery Scratcher, $5000 per week for 25 years."* Everything around me seemed to blur. Almost as if reality itself had suddenly slipped away, leaving me in a fantasy land. With that amount of money, I felt on top of the world. It was definitely a jarring experience, which I will never be able to forget. I continued to read the email, and it directed me to claim the winner's form and submit it to the California Lottery regional office.

My first plan of motion was to call my wife, Trina, and break the unbelievably good news.

"Trina, baby, you won't believe what I have to say," I shouted.

"What is it, Alex? And why are you shouting? Is Brandon okay?" Trina asked.

"Yeah, Brandon is completely fine, Trina, baby. You have WON the LOTTERY!" I exclaimed, and as soon as I said that out loud to my wife, I burst into tears of happiness. It was extremely sentimental and heartwarming. Tears were flowing down my cheeks, and each droplet was a testament to all that Trina and I had been through. My heart swelled with indescribable joy and satisfaction because there was nobody else I wanted to win the lottery with other than my partner, Trina.

"Trina, you're now a millionaire, and you won't have to work a day in your life anymore," I added.

"WHAT? No, WHAT? Alex. I can't. Are you for real?" Trina whispered. Trina's laughter mingled with loud sobs on the phone, a symphony of emotions that took over her as well.

"Yes, baby!! Now get home! We have to celebrate. I'm just on my way to get champagne so we can celebrate," I said.

Trina sniffled her happiness and tears and made her way home before her shift at the restaurant even ended.

I asked Trina to sit down, take a breather, and then broke the good news. I proceeded to tell her that she had WON the lottery, that now she was a millionaire, and that she didn't have to work another day in her life.

Chapter Two — Fran

Trina came home in a blink of an eye. Despite her shift timings that had not even ended, she came back home to congratulate me. I immediately got up and ran downstairs toward the entrance. I saw the car turning into our driveway, and I put on whatever shoes I could find by the staircase and ran toward the door. As soon as Trina got out of the car, I saw her face, which was a little puffy and red. I'm assuming it was because she could've gotten a little sentimental. Trina's radiant smile illuminated under the glistening sun while she couldn't stop smiling. Trina's contagious smile lit my entire day up, the pure and unfiltered smile that I always yearn to see. Trina's smile is infectious; her smile spreads warmth and brings my heart so much happiness and contentment. I paused for a second to just look at the love of my life and observe her in her immersed bliss. Her eyes sparkled with hints of tears rolling down.

She left all her belongings in the car and came running toward me. In pure elation, I ran toward the courtyard, and with each stride, the distance between us shrank up real fast. I hugged her. Her emotions were palpable, radiating pure elation and immense happiness and relief. Unable to contain the sheer magnitude of her joy, it was as if a tough weight had been lifted off her shoulders, allowing her spirit to soar freely.

In that moment of celebration, I enveloped her so tightly in an embrace, and at that moment, time seemed still. The hug was more than just a physical gesture; it was a pat on the back for all that we have endured in this life while having one another by our side. A definite testament to our intertwined happiness. As our arms were wrapped around one another, I could sense a palpable rush of relief and excitement pulsating through Trina and me. It was as if the universe paused for a second so that we could celebrate the sheer joy of this moment. It wasn't because we had just gotten so rich or that money was what united us, although it was because of all the countless hours and hard work that we had put into our lives to provide for one another and our son Brandon. The financial stress that we were constantly under completely ends today. Trina and I exchanged a hug for a good two minutes, and I could just hear her heart thumping fast.

"I still can't believe it, Alex. We did it. We actually DID it. Who would've thought?" She sniffled under her breath.

"I know, baby. It all feels so surreal. And you didn't even listen to the best part about it. We are the winners of not just ONE million dollars, but FIVE!!" I said excitedly.

"Holy moly!!! Alex, are you for real? This is a dream that just keeps on getting better and better." She shouted. "I- I don't know what to say…"

"I know, right??? Like, what did we do to deserve this?" I said. Trina was too stunned to speak; her mouth was left wide open.

"I cannot wait to tell my family about this. I simply can't wait to travel the world with you, Alex!!" Trina said.

With the weight of financial burdens lifted from our shoulders, living a simple life in Miami seemed very boring. Yes, that was one thing Trina and I had wanted to do for a long time. We wanted to travel the world, but with our options being very limited in the past, we were unable to travel most of the time. However, now we can travel wherever our hearts desire. Our hopes and dreams that we once dreamt of didn't seem so extraordinary anymore. They felt achievable and easy to pertain to. I guess that's the beauty of accessible cash. My heart was feeling extremely content, while my heart seemed to remain grounded. Despite all this money flowing in, I knew that we still had to remain practical and not get too carried away. I have a few plans and real estate that I want to invest in. However, Trina and I were sure about one thing, and that was to be smart about our money.

A few days passed when Trina and I finally headed out and completed the winner's form. We had to drive out to the closest regional lottery office, which was located in Hayward, California. As soon as we got there, it became more and more real. The regional lottery's building was somewhat of a weathered building that bared marks of age and use within a corporate landscape. As soon as we arrived, there were three regional officers waiting for us, eager upon our arrival. They escorted us to the backroom of the building and asked Trina and me to verify our identities.

They asked for our passports, ID cards, driver's licenses, and all the lottery tickets that we had purchased in the past. And also the winning lottery ticket that was the winning lottery raffle. It was as if we were being detained and caught in such serious illegal activity and that we had just been caught. Claiming our lottery prize was extremely stressful and demanding. The lottery officials were not friendly, and yes, this is coming from a probation officer. They told Trina and me to remain seated in the backroom of the building, which was very congested and hot. A brief period later, the three lottery officials came back in and interviewed us, asking us what our plans were and how we were supposed to spend this newfound wealth.

I said to them, "We are going to take a month- long vacation so that we can wrap our minds around all this that is happening." The lottery officials were a little intimidating and daunting, but they listened carefully to what we had to say. They proceeded to ask if we would like to participate in the media, have our photographs taken, and be featured in the local newspapers. Trina and I declined almost instantly, considering all the horror stories we have heard of people winning the lottery and coming forward in the public eye. We decided to stay anonymous during the entire process, and they happily agreed to abide by our wishes. Toward the end of our interview, one of the lottery officials asked me whether we would prefer a monthly payment of $2500 for 25 years or a huge influx in our bank account at once. I turned to the official and said, "I will leave this decision up to my wife, as I don't want to be responsible if I end up making the wrong decision."

The following months were a breeze. Trina and I decided to tell our families and close friends about the cash prize. They were all ecstatic about this life- revolutionary change and the new chapter that was ahead. We proceeded to live our lives as normal, although I made sure to go heavy on the groceries. I ventured off to the grocery store with no budget in mind; I traversed through each aisle, where my cart of items piled up into a huge mountain. I picked out the fresh produce in all categories, including packaged goods, snacks for Brandon and me, baked goods, and essentials that we needed for the month.

It was a treat! Although I have to admit, the entire bill was also pretty hefty. Well, what can I say? A way to a man's heart is his food!

The following week, when I returned to work at the Probation Department, I never spoke a word to my co-workers about it because I wanted everything to seem normal. Regardless of nothing actually feeling the same, at times, I just wanted to get up and leave because there was no point in doing this job anymore. However, one day, my co-worker, Chris Martin, and an acquaintance randomly announced, "Someone named Adam Jones had won $2500 per week for 25 years in the California Lottery. Man, what a lucky guy." It was exceptionally uncalled for, and I had to fight myself to keep my laughter in. It was so hard not to tell Chris about all the bizarre events that are happening in my life right now. Even though Chris always had my best interests at heart, my wife and I promised each other that we wouldn't tell extended family or friends because then that is how people would start using us. Although Chris has always been a bugger, he just wouldn't let go! And his suspicions were getting the best of him, so he confronted me one day.

He asked me, "Alex, you seem to be in a great mood these past few days, and since that article has come out, you have an even better mood. So what's the deal? And don't you dare lie to me; you know I know you damn too well." I didn't have it in me to lie to Chris, so I caved in and confessed! I begged Chris to keep it a secret since I wanted to stay anonymous throughout the entire process.

A few months passed, and just like that, $2.785 million was deposited into my bank account. Our lives became opulent overnight, with a staggering bank account that transformed our reality. With money out of the question, Trina, Brandon, and I decided to take a trip to Vietnam, Asia, to meet my father-in-law. I had never met him before, which is why it was sort of a big deal. Brandon was just a year old, although he turned out to be the sweetest baby on the flight. We planned to visit Rach Gia, which was Trina's birthplace and where she spent her adolescent years. Rach Gia came to me as a delightful surprise, a vibrant city nestled in the heart of Vietnam, which came with lots of cultural heritage and history. I will never forget the spicy Pho and Chuoi Nep Nuong pudding I had, which was divine. The food in Rach Gia was phenomenal, and I will never be able to forget it. The burst of flavors and spices that indulge in your mouth is lovely.

With Rach Gia's warm climate, my family and I got a little sunburnt. Although it was a delight to finally meet my in-laws and Trina's extended family. The kindness and warmth that I felt in his home were like no other. Laughter echoed through the space while we clinked our glasses of wine. I sat there for hours on end, bonding with him and telling him all about myself. From shared interests to tales of cherished memories, the evening unfolded, and we had a great meal together. As the day progressed, the consensus was unanimous. The bond that Bruce and I shared not only united our hearts but also forged a lifelong companionship.

The anticipation and anxiety that came with meeting Bruce was uncanny. I didn't want my father- in-law not to like me. He's a huge part of Trina's life; therefore, I wanted to make a good impression, too. The moment I met him, it was as if I was meeting somebody I'd known for years. As we gathered, we bonded over many things. We spoke about politics, the current day economy, how life is so different in the United States, and, of course, Trina. The moment Bruce met Brandon, it was love at first sight. He wrapped his arms around Brandon and handed him a red envelope, just for good luck and prosperity. He continued to give advice to Trina, telling her that she should give back to the community and feed the poor. I couldn't agree more; I believe that if we have been blessed with this amount of money, giving back to the poor should definitely be on top of our list. We spent two weeks visiting small monasteries and orphanages, donating thousands of dollars to many temples throughout Vietnam. Trina and I often went to the local market and purchased kilos of raw rice and staple foods to disperse to villagers in the surrounding areas of Rach Gia. We were jet-setting across the globe without a second thought. We parted ways with Trina's ancestral home and headed toward the States. Upon our return, we got a little side-tracked and made a pit stop in Dubai. Trina, Brandon, and I spent four beautiful days in Dubai before real life hit us back home.

Upon returning home, Trina and I vouched to invest in real estate and startups that we saw potential in. We planned on purchasing nine rental properties in the best places in Miami for additional income. The nine properties include family homes, duplex flats, and a fourplex for sharing. These properties themselves produced over fifteen thousand dollars a month in rental income. We also hired a property manager in Northern California who managed all our rental income, maintenance, and estate portfolio. The future definitely seemed bright for our family since Trina and I were significantly financially secure from our earlier financial windfall.

Toward early August, I recall having a heart- to-heart conversation with Trina about how we are to move forward in life. Thankfully, I was extremely content with where I was in my life. I finally took the plunge and decided to retire from my job and spend time with my one-year-old and Trina. I had just turned 50 years old, and it was time the old man got the chance to relax and become the couch potato I had always envisioned becoming. Our daily schedules consisted of me watching TV shows, drinking beer, and eating the best meals that I could find. I spend time with my son, Brandon, while Trina would usually be busy with friends or running errands.

You know that saying, "*People love to ruin beautiful things…*" Well, that's what happened with Trina and I. After living our lives in peace for almost nine months, Trina began to tell her friends about winning the lottery. Trina's best friend and confidante, Tran, was the first person Trina called and told about the good news. Tran is a lovely soul, and I got to know myself after she became extremely close to Trina. Trina would always invite Tran over, cook meals together, and even take her out for short weekends. At times, we would ask Tran to babysit Brandon for us when it was our usual date night. Trina and Fran were extremely close, just like two peas in a pod. However, when Fran heard about Trina and me winning the lottery, her entire demeanor toward us, including Brandon, changed. The news of our lottery win seemed to cast an unexpected shadow over Fran's unusual demeanor, which changed the dynamics between us all, including my son, Brandon. I was unable to grasp Fran's complex toward our good news. It was as if she was in a touch of disbelief. There was a noticeable shift in her interactions, where her behavior and emotions were difficult to decipher. It was almost as if the wind had a change of direction, where there was unspoken uncertainty lingering in the air.

In the blink of an eye, the peace and security that we were thriving on completely began to crumble. There was so much unexpected uncertainty and tension for no reason. Tran began to visit our house way too often, and at times without any warning either. She would make up false situations like, *Oh, my car stopped working, so I decided to drop by* or *Trina, let's have a games night, and let's make sure it's just us.* There was this one incident where we left her at our house to babysit Brandon, and when we returned home, she was found in our bedroom. It was so strange, and she used the *bathroom* excuse as bait. Tran began to do these strange things that made me question her behavior at times. I was always so suspicious of her actions, and I told Trina about her strange behavior, too, although she said that she was just acting unusually because a lot was going on back home. Small quirks started to surface, small incidents that didn't quite align with how she usually was before.

My wife is too naïve; Trina's issues lie in her inclination toward trusting and seeking positivity and goodness in others, making her highly susceptible to manipulation and consistently placing her utmost trust in the wrong individuals who always prove to be unreliable and untrustworthy. Trina and I would get into arguments and fights about Tran, and she would always get irritated as soon as I brought her up. Another strange situation that took place regarding Trina was that one day, I caught her snooping in our house, in a place where she had no business being.

I found Tran taking pieces of my wife's clothing without permission. She took a used shirt that was lying in the laundry basket and put it in her bag. I found that extremely unusual, and I told my wife about it. Trina had no idea that Tran did that, so she confronted her. She asked Tran why she couldn't possibly have taken her used T-shirt, and in her defense, she said to my wife, "Oh, Trina, I told you that I would borrow this shirt. You must've forgotten." To which my wife couldn't really say anything. However, who just picks up a plain old navy blue T-shirt and stuffs it in their bag? It is so strange. After my wife confronted her, Tran sort of freaked out and frantically left our home. That night, Trina and I had the biggest fight we have had in a while. She thought that I was being incredibly rude to Tran and that I should apologize.

Trina accused me of *changing* since we got this wealth and that I always jump to conclusions and accuse people of stealing from us and using us. Nevertheless, that's not the case. I have never been rude or arrogant toward anyone I've previously known. If anything, I have just put my boundaries a little higher, considering all the family members who constantly want to meet up with me now. That evening, our argument escalated pretty fast, and some rude things were being said to the point of extreme volume that Brandon woke up. I was taken aback by Trina's sudden words toward me, especially considering our shared history. It was shocking to see her this heated since it seemed influenced by her friend, whom I have never particularly been fond of.

Toward the beginning of 2015, our dynamics with Fran got so weird and strange that I knew for a fact that she did not have my best interest at heart. Fran's persistent involvement in my wife's and I's relationship became a nuisance. She seemed to manipulate and intentionally get involved in our family matters. Inserting her unnecessary opinions and presence when they weren't even sought. Despite my constant efforts to maintain boundaries, she persisted in getting herself involved in our lives. It was hard for Trina to live a peaceful life with Fran's presence because she became extremely toxic and draining. Fran had become so evil, toward February, she made an ultimate plan to rob my wife and me of our $5 million for her own guilty conscience.

Chapter Three — Five Million Dollars

Despite all of Fran's efforts to sabotage our lives, Trina and I were doing surprisingly well. We sat down and had a very much-needed conversation, and we spoke about everything that was bothering us. I decided to have this conversation right in the morning since we had a heated argument last night. I woke up extra early and tiptoed into the kitchen while Trina was still snoring. I measured the ratio of coffee grounds and carefully selected the beans that Trina adores. I used the locally roasted coffee beans that Trina loves to pick out from our nearest Trader Joe's and began the process. The freshly ground beans filled the aroma as I began to pour the vanilla syrup and fresh milk into the frother. I added extra vanilla syrup into Trina's mug because she likes her coffee extra sweet. I took out her favorite mug, which is a dainty ceramic mug with hand-painted Vietnamese- inspired flowers on it. She never really uses this mug, although I made sure to grab it from the back of the cupboard to make sure she appreciates the tiny gestures. As I began to stream the coffee into our mugs, I heard the stairs creak and heard Trina come down the stairs.

"Good morning, Baby. What's happening?" Trina asked while paving her way down the stairs. She had her fuzzy morning robe on while she scanned the entire living room and kitchen.

"Morning! I'm just preparing some breakfast for both of us," I said with a little hesitation.

"Uh… How come, Alex?" Trina said. Surprisingly, I could see her eyes gleaming. I mean, she does cook for me all the time. I love Trina's cooking so much.

"I'm not sure, baby. I just wanted to make you a good ol' English breakfast!" I said.

Trina looked at me and said, "Hey, hey, let's not get too ahead of ourselves and take note of bellies!" And she was right: I am gaining weight, which needs to be controlled ASAP!

"Alright, I'll make your avocado and toast, Trina!!" I muttered.

After making breakfast for my beautiful wife, we sat down at our dining table, and I decided to address yesterday night's heated argument. I was extremely apologetic and understanding and told Trina that Fran was truly a problem. I voiced all my concerns about how Fran was bothering me, and Trina took it really well. I said, "Look, I understand that Tran is your friend, although I believe her intentions toward you are not the best. It's fine to have friends, although there is a thin line between friendship and trespassing into your marriage. And I believe that that is what she was trying to do. I mean, look, Trina, we are so blessed. I'm not trying to say money is everything, but things have really turned out for the better for us. And, just because of one person and all that she has to say is ruining our mental peace and well-being."

Trina continued eating her breakfast and nodded her head the entire time.

"Look, Alex, I really appreciate you sitting me down like this and communicating with me rather than throwing shade and yelling at me. I don't appreciate it," Trina said.

"Hmm," I said, hoping that she was going to say something else after this.

"Although, I also realize that Fran is genuinely turning into a problem. I should've listened to you only a few days ago. You're not the only one who thinks this. I think so, too," Trina conveyed. As soon as she said this, I instantly felt a sudden relief. I wasn't going crazy after all.

"Yeah, exactly, baby. And every time you take her side, I end up feeling so helpless and start thinking as if I'm the one that's crazy!" I finally poured my heart out, and Trina and I were back to normal. Thank God. I had my wife back.

The following week, after having this discussion with Trina, these were some of the best weeks we had ever had together. Trina distanced herself from Fran, and she wasn't allowed to stroll into our house whenever she desired. Trina was very sweet about it. She told her that her family was visiting and that they were staying at our house. To which Fran had to give us space. When Trina and I fought over Fran and were finally over the entire situation, I decided to surprise Trina with a trip to Hawaii. Since Brandon has summer vacation, I decided what the perfect time is to book a trip to Hawaii during summer break.

We have never been to Hawaii, which is why it was so exciting and adventurous. With precise planning and a genuine heart brimming with excitement, I orchestrated this unforgettable surprise for my wife and son. Keeping it under wraps for weeks, I finally revealed the surprise with a handwritten letter and a brochure nestled right under her pillow. When Trina read the letter and saw the Hawaii brochure, she was ecstatic. She was over the moon and astonished. Trina's eyes danced in disbelief and exhilaration because I knew how much she wanted to go to Hawaii. She has always wanted to go. It was so funny because she didn't even get sorta mad at me for planning this. She went along with the plan and didn't question anything.

The next ten days were pure bliss. I planned a trip to stay four days in Maui, four days in Honolulu, and two days in Kauai. The moment we landed in Maui was remarkable; I was mesmerized by the bespoke beauty of the place. The lush landscapes, crystal blue waters, and golden sunsets had me mesmerized. I really maxed out my credit card's day limit by booking the 'Four Seasons Resort.' Trina didn't know that we were staying at one of the most expensive resorts in the world at the time of our arrival. We reached quarter to 12 at noon and headed straight toward the hotel. As soon as we landed, we were greeted by many people greeting us with cheerful smiles and wrapping colorful Lei all over us. They had one for Baby Brandon, too! We all felt so special in the moment. There was a lavish Mercedes convertible to pick us up from the airport, with our personal chauffeur ready to escort us to the hotel. As soon as we sat in the car, Trina shut the door, and before the chauffeur was even finished putting our luggage in the trunk, she thudded her purse onto me and said "Alex!! What is all this? What happened to keeping everything on the down low? I thought we were spending all our money WISELY!" she tried to whisper.

"Trina, take a chill pill! We're in Hawaii. Go big or go home!!" I said.

Trina rolled her eyes and looked out the window. I knew that she was in too good of a mood to complain. We drove across the luscious green fields, neighboring the stunning crystal blue waters. I rolled down the window to get a breath of fresh air, and the tranquility and serenity that I felt at that moment was uncanny. The gentle rustle of palm trees serenaded my soul in a complete state of relaxation. There was an undeniable sense of aloha spirit in the air, almost the perfect welcoming atmosphere. Maui's vibe was a seamless blend of good vibes and a complete sense of calmness.

When we reached the hotel, Trina was in utter shock. She was so surprised that she didn't know how to act. She has been wanting to stay at the 'Four Seasons' for as long as I can remember, and I was so glad that I booked it for our trip. We entered the luscious resort, and I was in awe of everything that surrounded me. The resort welcomed us with open arms into a paradise of tranquility and luxury. The hospitality in the resort was uncanny, from serving us Rose the moment we arrived to a welcome breakfast waiting for our arrival. As soon as we stepped into the concierge, there were so many people from different nations, which was so refreshing to see. I met people from all across the world, and they were all so sweet.

I had planned our first day in Maui, and we decided to go to Honolua Bay, which is about a 20- minute drive north of Lahaina. Not that far from our hotel, Honolua Bay is enclosed by luscious green cliffs that unveil the serene beauty of the crystal blue waters. It's definitely a destination that one needs to see with their own eyes. We took a day trip here, and Trina and I decided to swim. I rented snorkeling gear from a shack nearby and decided to explore the marine life of Hawaii. When I tell you that I was mesmerized, I am not even trying to exaggerate. The first plunge I took into the crystal clear waters was like a rush of emotions and sensations. I was not exactly sure how to feel. I was enthralled, but at the same time, I was emotional. The first marine life creature that I spotted was a sea turtle swimming far away from me; then, to my right, suddenly came the colorful fish swimming away in herds. I was so overwhelmed by the bespoke beauty of the place. The silence underwater, broken only by the south of my loud chanting breath with the rhythm of the sea, made my experience a thousand times worth everything. Even now, as I'm writing this book, I am unable to find the right words to express everything that I felt when I was underwater. Trina kept photographing pictures to post on Facebook and a couple pictures with the beautiful landscapes at the back. She showed all her friends on Facebook that we were in Hawaii for a family trip.

We stayed in Hawaii for a good nine days; it was nine days of beaches, massages, great food, and the best company. I urged Trina to go for those fancy massages because they are impeccable in Hawaii, and so she did. Waking up to the Hawaiian waters was pure bliss, with fresh juices and fruits served to us in the lavish complimentary breakfast. Haha, not gonna lie. I looked forward to the breakfast over there the most. It was one of the best breakfast spreads I have ever witnessed. Trina and I were definitely in our honeymoon period, with each passing day in Hawaii wrapping us in the embrace and leaving us with incredible and wholesome memories. These glorious memories will always hold a special place in my heart.

We got back home after nine long days in paradise, and the moment we arrived, it didn't feel normal. We were feeling FOMO from Hawaii and wanted to go back as soon as we arrived. I recall the night we got back, nothing at home was functioning properly. First, the bathroom's toilet was clogged, which left a nasty smell and filled up our house. It was so gnarly that Baby Brandon even started weeping because of it. Since we arrived late at night, it was almost midnight when we came, so no plumber or maintenance guy was ready to come to our house to fix the clogged pipe. I was immediately in a bad mood, where I was just irritated and hyper. Trina kept nagging me on and started things like getting a grip and fixing this. I was so jet-lagged that this was the last thing that was on my mind. So, we had a new fight. I shouted at her, and Trina wasn't expecting it one bit. Another thing that added to the cherry on top was that the AC in our master bedroom stopped functioning out of the blue. I mean, what an abysmal welcome back home, right?

A few days' back home, things were back to normal when, all of a sudden, I heard the doorbell. I was lying down on the couch when I shouted "Coming!" because I thought it was my Indian food takeout! Trina wasn't home, as she was visiting her cousins, who had been visiting the States after ten years, for dinner. I walked toward the door when I saw Fran's car in the driveway. My heart instantly plummeted as I caught Fran standing right at my doorstep since this was the last person that I thought would show up at our house. At this point, I wasn't sure what I should do as she had heard me, and I couldn't even act like I wasn't home because she had seen our corridor's lights on, which implied that somebody was definitely home. I felt frightened. It took me a good two minutes to reach the door and open it. With a lot of hesitation, I opened the door, and Fran was standing there with a big bouquet of flowers and a bag of goodies. She was beaming with an evil grin, almost reaching her ears.

"Hey, Alex. How are you?" she said. It was so fake that I wanted to shut the door on her face.

"Hi, Fran. I'm alright. Trina isn't home, so do you want to come back later?" I asked.

"Oh no, it's alright! I can wait, and why don't you brew me a nice cup of green tea?" Before I even said anything, Fran paved her way into the door, finding her way to our living room. I was so annoyed.

"So Alex… Where is Trina? And how was Hawaii? I'm so hurt that you guys didn't tell me before leaving," Fran said while scanning our entire

house as if she were an FBI agent. With an air of utter curiosity, Fran stepped into our home and stared at everything with unusual intensity. Every corner of our house seemed to draw her attention, where her evil gaze lingered on the tiniest of details. Her manner and audacity were slightly unnerving, almost as if a detective was piecing something together.

"Oh, you know her cousins, Allison and Bree? They're here from Vietnam after ten years. So she's gone to meet them."

"Okay, and also, how was Hawaii? How long were you guys there for? And where did you stay? It looked fancy," she questioned.

I knew that I had to be pretty careful with my words, so I kept it as brief as I could.

"Um, Hawaii was great. I had the best time with Trina and Brandon, and we made lots of friends," I said.

"Okay, but where did you stay? It looked extravagant," she questioned again.

"We stayed at the Four Seasons resort. Yeah, it was really nice," I said in a very awkward way. I mean, who asks that? It's just so weird. She's so persistent. "Okay, Fran, are you going to head outside or wait for Trina because she might be a little late."

"No, I'm okay, Alex. I'm just going to wait for Trina to head back. I'll say hi and then leave!" she said.

"Alright, let me whip up a cup of green tea for you."

I headed toward the kitchen to make Fran a cup

of green tea and tried to waste as much time as I could because I didn't want to come and make fake talk with her. I had a glimpse of Fran from the living room, and she was just acting strange in general. I had a feeling that something was extremely suspicious. I turned around to grab a mug from the cupboard, and when I turned around, she was nowhere to be found. My heart dropped instantly. The worst possible things were going through my head at once. My first instinct was, where's Brandon? He should be sleeping in his cot upstairs, but I had the baby monitor in the kitchen. And all seems to be quiet in his room. So thank God she didn't go to his room to get him or something. I had a feeling that she was just going to take Brandon away; I don't know why. Although I shouldn't be thinking like this, because it is Fran, after all. Regardless of how she has been acting, I don't think she is capable of KIDNAPPING someone's child. That's cruel.

I'm not sure why I thought that.

I collected myself together and continued making Fran her green tea. After five minutes, she came back into the living room and sat back down. I'm assuming that she went to the bathroom, although it was strange because she went with the bag of *goodies* she brought to our house. I gave her the cup of green tea and sat down in front of her. There were many periods of silence, although I put on the news in order to break any awkwardness. I believe that Fran definitely has an idea that I'm not her biggest fan. In the meantime, I heard the driveway open, and I was praying to the gods that it was Trina. I immediately got up to check and collected her from the back door.

"Trina, Fran is over. Just warning you."

"Oh gosh? How come? That's so unusual of her. What does she want?" she asked.

"I'm not sure, actually. She wants to meet you," I said while rolling my eyes.

We made our way to the living room, and there Fran was, sitting with her cup of green tea, watching the news. She turned around toward Trina and got up to give her a hug. I almost felt bad.

"Hey, Girl!!! How have you been? It's been a long time, Trina. How was Hawaii? Tell me everything," she said.

Trina gave her a big hug as well.

"No, it was amazing! Alex surprised me. I didn't even know; it was all so last minute. I barely had time to shop or even pack! What have you been up to?" Trina replied.

"I'm good, I'm good. Is that a new ring?" Fran asked as her eyes scoured Trina.

"Uh. Yeah, it is. Alex bought it for me."

Fran's entire demeanor changed after that. It was as if something compelled her, and she was not able to digest the fact that Trina was wearing a hefty- sized diamond cut ring that was breathtaking.

"You know, I believe that you need to relax a little with your money. Like, I get it; it's all exciting and amazing to have a great amount of wealth in your bank accounts, but just know that it's bound to finish like this," Fran said in an envious manner. It was rude.

"Fran, I appreciate your concern, but what my wife and I decide to do with our money is our personal matter. Thanks," I said in a very polite way.

"Watch your mouth, Alex. I'm talking to my friend here," Fran blurted.

"Excuse me? Don't talk to me like that. She is my wife at the end of the day," I retorted.

"Fran, don't speak to my husband like that. And what he's saying is right; I mean, it's none of your concern what we do and what we don't do," Trina said in our defense. I couldn't stand the lady's face any longer, so I left them and headed upstairs. I felt like shouting at something and taking out all my anger and frustration.

A few moments later, Trina came upstairs to get ready for bed. I asked her what Fran's deal was, and even Trina was unable to understand. The conversation between us downstairs was about to get a little heated. However, I held myself back and decided not to say anything because then I would have said some rude things that I would regret saying later. As I was ready to head to bed, Trina was doing her nighttime routine, and I asked her if Fran said anything after I headed upstairs so abruptly.

"Nope, she ignored it. Although she was persistent in me trying her brownies that she made herself. I mean, Alex, I was so full, and she literally forced me to take a bite of the brownies she'd left me. She kept saying that they're homemade and stuff."

"How were they? Strange, she didn't offer me the brownies? And I was sitting with her for a good thirty minutes. LOL."

"Hahahahaha, I'm not sure, Alex, I don't think she likes you very much!"

We called it a night and snuggled into bed. I was grateful. I am grateful, after all.

Chapter Four — Victor

Trina was extremely ill for the past two weeks, and I'm not quite sure what went wrong. My heart ached as I recall the days when she was on constant bed rest for a week straight. It consumed her entire being and left me in a state of profound anxiety and sheer terror. Brandon and I were missing Trina's presence so much that our house felt completely empty and desolate. Trina battled an illness that seemed to drain the essence of her vitality. It started with a fever that burned within her, which was followed by a gnarly and persistent cough that weakened her even more. After self-treating herself with mild drugs, Trina found herself battling a depilating stomach infection that gripped her entire body with relentless intensity. She was feeling nauseous constantly, with sharp stabbing pains in her left abdomen that doubled her suffering.

I called the doctor home twice to get her fever sorted, although the doctor said that she might need to be hospitalized in case her health deteriorates. I was not sure how bad Trina's health got, although seeing her like this certainly made my heart break. Since my baby doesn't deserve any of this. I remember going to the hospital, where the doctor called me in and told me that she was also unable to find the core cause of this illness. Which had me worried sick to my stomach. I mean, how much longer would Trina have to suffer like this. I asked the doctor how long Trina would be suffering like this, and she said that since we don't have an exact idea of what caused this illness, it might take longer to recover. She prescribed more medicine. I had to look after Brandon all on my own. He craved his mother's warmth, love, and attention, which I was unable to give him. That month was definitely a whirlwind of emotions, where, at times, I felt like crumbling into tiny pieces, and at other moments, I just felt like crying because home wasn't the same anymore. The home, which I consider my safe haven, was abruptly disturbed. I mean, after Hawaii and the best ten days of our life, this is what we got struck with.

During the time of Trina's illness, I realized the true importance of my wife. Don't get me wrong, I love my wife more than words could describe, although, after this altercation, I have now realized that Trina is my safe haven. Every time I come home, I look for her, which brings my heart the peace it craves. Seeing my baby like that wasn't bringing me any sort of comfort, although I was eternally grateful that God didn't take her away from me. Every time friends and family came to visit, they were utterly shocked to see Trina like this because she had become so weak. Her persistent fever and unyielding pain were a ceaseless battle against the ailment that drained her vitality day by day. Once, Trina walked into a room and lit the entire place up, leaving behind a frailty and anemic body, which I pray to the Lord she recovers from. It took Trina a good month to properly recover. I remember there were many nights when I had to get up from my sleep and sing lullabies to Brandon, comfort him, and make him go to bed. Thankfully, I had hired a babysitter to look after Brandon when I was called in for work.

Approximately a month later, Trina was back on her feet. Her recovery process required heaps of medicine bills and visits to the doctor. I can only wonder what people do when they're tight on budget. How do they manage when a loved one is sick?

Because medical expenses are so expensive. The hospital loves to just cash people out, and what if people are actually sick? And they don't have the funds to afford the proper medicine and care? My heart goes out to them. Thankfully, due to the lottery money that we were blessed with, it was easy to pay for Trina's medical bills. When Trina was feeling much better, all her friends decided to surprise her with a picnic in our backyard. Since it was almost springtime, her friend Cassidy decided that all the girls brought one dish that Trina loved to eat. Cassidy asked me just to provide them with some drinks and supplies that are required for this picnic. She even volunteered to pick Brandon up from his daycare, which I happily agreed to.

I took out the summer rugs and all the picnic utensils that were required for this picnic from the ancient attic that resided in the strangest corner of our house. With this excitement, I wanted everything to be perfect because it's so sweet of Cassidy to think of something like this. She was in charge of the entire guest list, and I gave her full permission to call whomever she wanted. I yanked out the wicker basket that Trina had bought years back, which had never come to proper use before. I took our two large carpets that were dusty and rolled up all the way in the corner. They definitely had a run for my money because as I reached to pull them out, I heard my knees clack! Gosh.

I made sure to rake the garden, collected all the leaves, and dumped them into the dumpster outside. I laid the two large carpets so her friends could be comfortable. Then, I made sure to use two large bed sheets that were worn out on top of them. Hoping that Trina won't mind me using our bed sheets, you know. I set the picnic table with a sweet little cheese board from Trader Joe's, which I got on a bargain, followed by some red wine and roses. The picnic table looked very cute and presentable, and I know that Trina would be proud of my presentation skills. The guests began to arrive at quarter to 4, which gave me plenty of time to prepare. Brandon's babysitter had arrived, so I was just waiting for Cassidy to arrive.

Cassidy arrived at 4:15 with baby Brandon all caught up in her arms. Brandon was also in a chirpy mood, which put me in a great mood, too. I had told Trina to pick up Aunt Mary, whom everyone loves and cherishes, to bring home. Aunt Mary is such a sweet soul who spreads positive vibes all around. I told Trina to have her over because she has been quite proficient in Trina's recovery process. She made sure to drop by the hospital and hand Trina flowers despite her old age.

As the guests began to arrive, I placed a board hanging against the picnic table's wall, which said *Trina's Thriving!* which I DIY'ed out of Pinterest myself. I know Trina will definitely appreciate it. As her friends began to arrive, Cassidy went in with Beth to set up the food on the kitchen counter. I was inside the house to meet and greet all of Trina's friends when I caught a glimpse of Fran's car. That instant, I thought to myself, "Yikes, why is she here?"

I got myself busy with pulling out the wine glasses because I was in no mood to be fake. As soon as I saw Fran walking in, I saw a man walking in right behind her. The middle-aged man had salt and pepper hair, was neatly groomed, and seemed like he was ready for me. He was wearing stylish glasses that subtly conveyed his intellectual demeanor. His eyes were small, although they possessed a keen and discerning gaze that reflected the wealth of life experiences. Don't get me wrong, the man was dressed in impeccably tailored clothing; he was wearing a sleek white button-down, ironed to perfection, that accentuated his entire aura. Now, I don't really gawk at people like this, but just because he came with Fran, I was a little skeptical. I was in plain ol' beige shorts and a plaid shirt, which made me feel extremely undressed.

Since Fran never really used to introduce us to people like this, it was unusual to see her bring this fellow over to our place. He walked in with an expensive bottle of vine as a welcome present, and I paved my way through the bunch of fellows to greet them.

"Hey Fran, long time. How are you doing?" I said. I had to put on a sweet act because I didn't want to be rude. Fran surprisingly leaned in for a hug, which was kind of shocking considering the heated argument we had last time.

"Hi, Alex. I'm alright, how far is Trina? Let me introduce you to my friend Victor here. He's an old friend of mine, back from college," she said excitedly. Victor leaned in for a hug and handed me the bottle of wine.

"Hiiya! Alex, I have heard so much about you, and it's great to finally meet you. I hope it's not a problem for me to show up like this with Fran," Victor's voice was a little raspy; he was very cool, calm, and collected, which I liked.

"Not a problem at all, my man, please make yourself at home. Fran, you know where all the snacks are; please help yourself!" I was pleasantly surprised with Victor's warmth and amiability; he was definitely spreading positive vibes.

I grabbed Fran, Cassidy, Elizabeth, and Victor some wine glasses so we could get the party started. The girls hovered in one corner, and Victor was hovering around me the entire time.

"So what do you do for work? Are you from around the block?" I asked.

"No, actually, I live in San Francisco, which is not really a far drive from here. I have a couple of vineyards and estates that I look after my parents," Victor said.

"Oh, no way? That's honestly pretty cool! Is this vine from your vineyard?" I asked Victor let out a chuckle and said, "Yeah, it pretty much is. Let me know how you like it. I practically gift everyone a bottle of vine from my vineyard."

Victor's personality and aura were very calming and soothing. I had a wonderful time getting to know him as an individual, especially somebody who has traveled the world so much and has knowledge about almost every part of it.

Trina finally arrived, and as soon as she saw the driveway full, she knew that I was up to something. She parked her car outside our lawn, adjacent to the front door's entrance, and walked in. As soon as she walked into the house, she could see through the long window that was opposite the corridor and saw her best friends, Elizabeth, Cassidy, Fran, etc., sitting in the yard.

As Trina and Aunt Mary stepped out on the porch, her eyes widened in a joyful surprise, and her luminous smile beamed across her face. An unmistakable spark ignited in her eyes, which left her mouth wide open. Her heart swelled with sheer joy, and she couldn't contain the contagious laughter that was filling up in the air. At that moment, I knew that Trina was extremely happy; she was surrounded by positivity and love. Trina felt an overwhelming wave of love and gratitude pour all over her. As Aunt Mary entered alongside her, her thrill and excitement even surpassed Trina's. She clutched onto Trina's arm, smiling while looking at her, getting so happy. Aunt Mary held Trina so tightly, the affection she felt for her niece resonating from the very core of her being, a love that transcended any sort of description.

After meeting and greeting everyone, Fran introduced Victor to Trina. As the introduction was made, there was an immediate ease in the air, as if we had been friends for years. It was quite unusual; Victor was a very wonderful surprise. Conversations flowed effortlessly, and we spoke about our shared interests and the joy of newfound connections. From that day forward, the four of us became great friends and created a bond that we forged never to break. Since Victor was such a delight, I believe that all the bad thoughts I had about Fran were slowly disappearing, so I didn't mind seeing her in social gatherings again.

Trina, Fran, Victor, and I became close friends after the picnic I threw for Trina. We all started hanging out and became close friends, and it always felt like we were a family. Victor invited us to his humble abode quite a couple of times for either game night or poker, and Trina and I loved the vibes at his house. Victor was such a sweet lad, and he introduced us to his mom and sister as well. You see, it's hard to find like-minded people who get along with you after a certain period. I believe that with Victor, I did have a great friendship; he made me feel so comfortable about whatever it was that I was thinking. I was able to crack any sort of lame joke that I wanted to without any judgment involved. I remember that one time when my car got stuck on the main highway. I called Victor, and he was there in ten minutes. He called the maintenance guys, and he had it all figured out.

The first time I arrived at his lavish home, which was nestled atop a hillside in the heart of North California's wine county, Victor's lavish estate was the epitome of modern luxury and extravagance. He had a large car park, followed by two towering pillars that stood as stoic sentinels, entirely framing the entryway in an aura of regal magnificence. As soon as you entered his home, you would be greeted with higher ceilings and white marble embossed on every table and tile. The first time Trina and I went to his house, we were shocked at how expensive his lifestyle must be. I mean, keeping up with a house like this, especially trying to maintain it, must not be easy, nor cheap!

About three months into our friendship, when Victor invited us to his house for drinks, I assumed that his other friends would be there too. I was in the mood to socialize, although it was strange how it was just Fran, Trina, and I. It was always like this. I found it sort of strange how he never introduced us to his other friends since I believe Trina and I are cool. That night, I recall finding myself looking for the bathroom in Victor's huge house. His guest bathroom, which is situated on the first right alley of his main entrance, was under construction due to some plumbing issues. During this time, Trina, Fran, and Victor were in the middle of a heated poker game, where I was unable to hold and had to go to the bathroom desperately. As I found myself desperately looking for another bathroom, Victor shouted, "Alex!! Just go upstairs and turn to the right, and you'll find my room. Just go to the bathroom in there!"

I said, "Thank you!!" before proceeding to go up the stairs to find Victor's room.

As I clung onto the stairs to find myself in the bathroom, I was trying my best not to fall since I was very tipsy. I hurried toward Victor's room, which was a little different from my imagination. His room was very big, strangely large, and it was painted all black, which is an odd choice to paint your room like that. It sprawled out in an unexpectedly vast expanse, where the walls, ceiling, and even the floor bore the deep, inky shade of black that enveloped his entire room. Such a choice in color for your bedroom created an unusual ambiance that oscillated creepy vibes. His bed was situated in the corner of the room, right next to the big window, which was certainly odd considering the dimensions of the room. Everyone knows that you place the bed opposite or adjacent to your windows and across the bathroom.

Another thing that I noticed as soon as I walked into his room was the odd smell that was coming out of it. An unusual scent slinked out from within the room, just like an unexpected concoction that seemed hard to explain. Almost as if a hint of something sweet, reminiscent of vinegar, creating an unsettling yet oddly intriguing combination. It was mysterious for sure; I can only wonder how Victor lived in a place like this.

When I paved my way toward the bathroom, I caught a glimpse of Victor's bedside drawer, and I couldn't believe what I had just seen. It was a picture of Trina, Brandon, and I from Hawaii. My instant reaction was to take the picture down and punch the guy. Although, it took everything in me to fight my gut reaction and proceed as if I didn't see anything. I summoned every ounce of willpower to suppress my instinctive response, to hide any traces of my initial shock. But the moment I laid my eyes on this picture, a chilling wave of despair washed all over me, plunging my heart into the depths of my stomach. A sickening sensation gripped me tightly, with an unsettling blend of fear that sent shivers down my spine. I felt sick, I was scared, and there were droplets of sweat running down my face.

At that moment, a sense of dread and apprehension seized me, an overwhelming mixture of emotions that threatened to overwhelm my composure. I collected myself, used the bathroom, and headed downstairs. There were a million things that were constantly running through my head. I mean, *why* on earth would Victor, who is supposedly my friend, have a picture of my family and me in his room? What sort of game was he playing? Does he envy me and my family? Does he want to cause us harm? I mean, why else would he have that picture?

The only thought that was running in my mind was why certain individuals had pictures of other people. My first thought was that Victor had something to do with Black magic. I mean, I kept second-guessing myself and thinking that this was absurd. This is the sort of thing that we see in movies, and that is not possible in real life. I mean, I have never heard of black magic before. My mind was going through twenty things at the same time; I believed that Alex was genuinely a nice guy, and I thought he was a good friend to have, considering I don't have that many friends. I collected myself, used the bathroom, and headed downstairs.

When I headed downstairs, I told Trina to get up and that we were leaving. I was confused about whether to confront Victor right now, but I thought it was best not to say anything right now. Trina had just won the game of poker, and they all were sitting and egging her on; my face was red.

"Hey baby, let's go. We're leaving."

"What happened, Alex? Please give me a moment, Victo…."

"No, Trina, I don't want to hear it. Let's go!" I semi-shouted. My emotions were all over the place; they took over me.

"Don't talk to me like that," Trina got up, took her things, said bye to Victor and Fran, and stormed out.

"What's the matter, Alex?" Victor posed his question in a courteous demeanor, although tinged with an unusual touch. Fran already knew something was up, which is why she remained silent. I can never forget Fran's strange demeanor that night.

Trina and I drove home that day, and during that car ride, Trina lost it. In a sudden whirlwind of emotion, Trina's entire composure shattered, and a storm of frustration ignited within her. Her temper flared up like wildfire, and some really rude words tumbled out of her mouth.

"Alex, how insecure are you?" Trina shouted.

"Excuse me? I beg your pardon?" I said sarcastically.

"What is the matter with you? Every time I'm having a good time, you just want to storm out, regardless of anything that is going on. Is it Victor? Are you jealous?" she insinuated.

"No, Trina! Why would I be insecure because of Victor? *I don't care for Victor!"* I shouted. I had completely lost my temper, too.

"Calm down, baby. What's the matter? I thought you really liked Victor? You two are like close friends, right? And I always thought you had a great time having him around. What's gotten into you?" Trina asked politely.

"Trina, I believe that Victor isn't who I think he is."

"What do you mean? What happened?" Trina sensed the fright in my voice; she automatically knew that something was not right.

"When I…" I took a long breath and gasped, "When I went up to his room to use the bathroom, I saw something very strange in his bedside drawer. And the entire aura of his room was extremely strange and appalling."

"What did you see, Alex? Tell me right now!"

"I saw a picture of me, you, and Brandon printed on a large piece of paper. And… And… I don't know what to do with this; that is so strange, right? Trina, my heart shattered when I saw that. And the only thing that was going through my mind was *black magic.*"

Trina let out a sharp gasp, her voice caught in her throat, rendering her to be speechless. Her belief in Black Magic ran deep, rooted in her Asian heritage, where countless tales of black magic are echoed and heard from generations. I believe that this belief held an emotional weight for her, with countless amounts of stories and experiences that shaped her understanding of this gruesome doing.

"Alex, that is the number one thing an individual does in order to apply black magic on someone. What are we going to do?" Trina said while a stream of droplets rolled down her cheeks. She knew this was extremely dangerous and vile.

"I mean… What about Brandon?" she cried. "How is this any of his fault? I'm worried sick to the stomach for my baby."

I grabbed Trina's hand and grabbed it as tightly as I could. I wanted her to know that she was not alone in this.

"Trina, baby, I have got you. I have got baby Brandon as well. Now that we know, we are never seeing those crazy freaks ever again," I said.

"Yeah, but Alex, you don't understand. Black magic is evil. We have invited them to our house multiple times. It's not just something we can sit and ignore. I can't believe Fran. I mean, I gave her so many chances to change, and she never did. That sick lady repulses me," Trina said angrily.

"I know, baby. I know."

"ALEX, don't you remember when Fran also snuck a T-shirt of mine into her bag? That could be a form of black magic, too," Trina said, frightened, while tears came trembling down her face. I didn't know how to help her; I was worried myself.

We reached home, and both of us were overwhelmed with thousands of emotions. We didn't know what to do. I could sense how horrified Trina is now. Although, if anything, this gave me the lesson to *never* trust anyone ever again. I made the biggest mistake by letting some like Victor and Fran into our lives.

Trina called her father back home in Vietnam and told him exactly what I saw. Bruce was very understanding and knew exactly what to do. He told us not to worry and that he will handle this situation back home. All he told us to do was cut all ties with Victor and Fran and make sure to block them off from every social media platform. He advised Trina to get a burning sage and burn it around the entire house, which may get rid of evil spirits and any negative energy that has been left behind.

A few months later, approximately three months after Trina and I completely cut Victor and Fran out of our lives, I thought things would get better. However, after that night, I began to get extremely paranoid about everything, and it took a gnarly toll on Trina and my relationship. We both started fighting way too often and cussing each other out. I kept telling myself that this wasn't Victor and Fran's curse, but it was. It was the summer of 2022 when our lives went into shambles.

Trina decided to work at the local school nearby to pass the time while I was almost about to hit my retirement and get my pension. During this time, all our investments in Florida began to fail, and our real estate agent over there decided to scam us. It was as if there was a tragedy upon tragedy that Trina and I were not ready to confront. The duplex that we put up for rent had no bookings at all for the following year, thanks to COVID. The house we bought in Florida that had the most potential got flooded and taken over due to a natural disaster. Once I called up the real estate agent, he blocked me and never picked up my phone. I told Trina that I would be flying over to Florida to investigate matters over there and hire a lawyer who could deal with our issue and get the help we needed.

Trina did not find it safe for me to go to Florida, leaving her behind with Brandon. However, I was unable to find a better option as to what to do, considering the circumstances. I decided to leave for Florida since it was peak summertime, hoping that some potential buyers or rentals would take a chance and invest in our place. Due to the urgent and tragic circumstances, I recall my heart not being at ease when I left Trina and Brandon behind. I believe that I knew that things were about to get worse.

Chapter Five — My RV That Brought Us Nothing but Misery

After returning back home from Florida, I knew that things were certainly about to get bad. The lawyer that I decided to see in Florida was of no use. He said that in order to rent and sell properties, I would need an interstate license, which I didn't have. He said that it's mandatory for landlords to have an interstate property license in order to rent and sell properly. In order to rent and sell, Mark also said that I would need to travel from California to Florida far more regularly than coming out here once or twice a year. Flying out to Florida every other month seems a little expensive, which is why I'm thinking of investing in an RV; it would serve as a means to travel, sleep, and potentially even live while on the go. Although, I should definitely discuss this with Trina and then make a final decision on what I want to do.

The morning after reaching home, my mind was all over the place. I mean, my mind was constantly perplexed about all that was happening around us. I decided to sit Trina down and let her know that I would be investing in an RV and that it is a great opportunity for all of us to do interstate travel as a family. Trina was finishing up the laundry when I told her to come in and sit.

"Hey baby, can you get in here? I need an opinion," I said politely.

"Yeah, one sec!" Trina muttered.

"I'm thinking of buying an RV, considering all the interstate travel I will have to be doing through California to Florida. What do you think?"

"Um… I have never really thought that we were the type of family that would invest in an RV, hahaha. However, if you believe that it's a smart decision, financially and practically, then go ahead. I'm sure it will come in use for me as well later on," Trina muttered.

"Trina, you know that I have been wanting an RV for so long, so why not just get it now?"

"How much is it for, though? Alex, you know we need to start budgeting, especially after all the fancy-schmancy trips we have been taking. We even need to make Brandon a bank account and invest in his college tuition. I hope you know that," Trina said while glaring into my eyes.

"Yes, of course, I know that, don't worry."

"Alright, as long as we're on the same page about everything…."

I assured Trina that our money wasn't going to be wasted.

The following morning, which was a Saturday, I decided to take my buddy Walter from work to the largest RV dealer, which was situated thirty minutes outside town. Since it was peak summer time, RV dealerships were operating in full swing because this was the best time to invest in one. Mark and I arrived at the RV dealership and were very pleasantly surprised when we were greeted by a striking lineup of RVs neatly arranged in a single-file row. The sight was charming, with various models standing tall, all showcasing their unique features and style. They all differentiated from various price points, where some were very basic and dirt cheap, and others were exceedingly expensive beyond means. On one end, luxurious motorhomes radiated luxury and class with their sleek designs and expansive bodies. With polished and pristine exteriors and spacious interiors, it promises comfort and extravagance on the road. Moving along the line, we saw the Class C models, which seemed to strike a balance between the other categories. They boasted a different structure, minimizing space without compromising on maneuverability. The exterior of these RVs was not bad, although it was comfortable.

I decided to invest in a far more luxurious RV that stood in the corner, with an outstanding interior and a comfortable bed that was built in. This RV had a spacious interior that had an outstanding amount of space available. The built-in living area felt inviting and adorned with warmth, which created a cozy atmosphere. The intricately designed kitchen was instilled with modern appliances that were ready to cater to any culinary adventures that we were going to take. There was an ample amount of space to store our belongings, which included a massive trunk under the RV to store extra baggage. What sold me to buy this RV was the large windows and picturesque views that invited the natural sunlight to flood in during the day. Since RVs can get a little stuffy, I wanted to buy one that comes with large windows so that we could roll down the windows any time we needed. This RV, which I decided to call Bob, was a perfect balance between practicality, functionality, and comfort, which created an enticing haven for both travel and living.

I paid the RV seller with my AMEX, and I was ready to take the RV home. I had asked the seller if it was alright if I could park the RV here for a while, and he said yes. However, he also said that once it's out of his garage, he won't let me park it again. Basically, what he was trying to say is that I would need to figure out a parking space for the RV. I came home and showed Trina pictures of the RV; I was very proud of my findings. Trina seemed ecstatic about our future endeavors on this RV.

I spent the following days venturing off to the dealership, exploring the RV a little further. I took it out for a test drive, and it drove perfectly, where you couldn't even tell that I was driving an entire house. Since I drove out of the dealership, I needed to find a parking space as soon as possible since the dealership guy refused to let me in again. I even thought of parking it outside our house, although I knew that wasn't possible since it's a residential area and the neighbors would be super paranoid. However, there wasn't much choice. I had to park the RV outside our house till I found a permanent solution. I drove the RV home, and it was a treat. The size of the RV is a monstrosity, which was initially intimidating, but once I settled into the driver's seat and hit the road, it was pure exhilaration. The panoramic windshield offered an incredible view of the Californian sun, which made each mile an adventure in itself. It isn't just a vehicle; it is a mobile home, and every turn of the wheel felt a step closer to a new adventure.

I reached home and honked twice to tell Trina that I was home! She came outside after two minutes with baby Brandon, tugged above her waist.

"Honey! This is massive!" Trina blurted. It was supper time, so many of the neighbors were outside watching me park this in, too. They were also amazed by the monstrosity of this truck; a mini crowd started to form outside our driveway. Where I felt like a complete celebrity!

"Hop in, Trina. Let me show you around!" I felt like buying this RV was a good decision, and I felt extremely content about my purchase. I'm not sure why I thought that all the bad days were behind us when I purchased this. The neighbors also wanted to look inside the RV to see the pure luxury that I had just rolled in. I politely accepted their request and gave them their time to look around.

"Alex, you have definitely dropped a big buck on this!" one of the neighbors muttered.

"What can I say? The pension money is rolling in!" I said. They all started giggling, knowing that I was about to retire!

The RV was parked in our driveway for about a week when Trina got a complaint from the County Department that lots of residents were getting irritated by the parking. I mean, I understand since it was blocking the road behind. I knew that the residents around would complain sooner rather than later because it was hard for them to drive by their houses. Nevertheless, I wasn't sure where to park the RV since there weren't places to park an RV like this. If I were to park it at a random driveway, there were major risks of anyone breaking in. Therefore, I needed to be careful as to where I wanted to park my RV.

Two days later, while I was getting ready for work, Trina was preparing breakfast when she caught a glimpse of the RV, which was parked right outside our house. While she was brewing up some coffee, she saw that somebody had broken into the RV and that the windows on the left side of the RV were all smashed, with heaps of glass spread all around the driveway. She ran upstairs to tell me, and I was shocked.

"Alex!! Someone broke into our RV, and there's shattered glass everywhere," Trina mumbled in a panicked manner.

"What…? For the love of God! Can't I catch a break for once?"

"I'm not sure, but who do you think could have done this?" Trina asked.

"I don't know, man. Do you think the County Police would provide me the security footage?" I am keen on finding out who this could be. I had my own suspicions.

"Yes, I think you can. Do you want me to call Lauren? She's tight with Peter, who is the head of the department," Trina was very helpful, which I appreciated a lot.

"Yes, please, Trina. I have to go back to work, and I can't take any other bad news."

After tying up my shoelaces, I found myself hating everything high and sight. The world around me appeared in a different, irritable light, and a mad wave of dissatisfaction crept in. I mean, who could it be? Do we think it's Victor and Fran? I'm not sure. I mean, how could they have even known that I had gotten an RV? Were they sending negative and evil spirits?

My thoughts spiraled into a whirlwind of worst-case scenarios, each one more vivid and catastrophic than the last. I was sitting there on my bed, where dark shadows of uncertainty danced on the walls of my consciousness, painting a bleak picture of all the possibilities that could go wrong. A gut-wrenching pain started to occur in my heart, and I was giving it my all for the pain to stop. Although it wasn't, gradually, the pain spread from my heart to my left arm, causing me a lot of discomfort. The sheer intensity became unbearable, trapping me in a state of excruciating pain. Trina was nowhere to be found, so I sat there, overwhelmed with what was happening to me, feeling paralyzed by the severity of the situation. I recall my eyes slowly shutting and not being awake after that.

"Alex, Alex, ALEX," Trina shouted.

Trina's urgent concern ignited a forceful jolt, her hands pressed firmly against my shoulders, shaking me with a desperate urgency. Each nudge felt deliberate and with a lot of force, her touch carrying an intensity that conveyed the gravity of the moment. "Alex, WAKE UP. WAKE UP, Alex," she shouted again.

I gained consciousness and retorted back to her by moving my head. I was unable to speak at that moment. I responded to her by tilting my head back and forth, acknowledging her efforts. However, at that moment, I was unable to say anything. Upon waking up, the sight above me seemed oddly unfamiliar; the ceilings looked somewhat different. Gradually, it dawned on me that I was lying on top of a hospital bed. The realization trickled in like a hesitant realization of unexpectedness. The transition from my unconsciousness in the hospital made me shift my consciousness to reality really fast.

"Alex, how are you feeling? I've been worried sick. I rushed you to the hospital as soon as I saw you upstairs," Trina said while sobbing.

"Wait, what even happened?"

"You had a heart attack; thankfully, it was a minor one. I think it was because you found out that someone broke into your RV," Trina tried to crack a joke.

"Hahahahaha, don't make me laugh, Trina, it hurts."

A drip was connected to my left arm, feeding it into a bag that collected my blood. The drip, a passageway for this vital fluid, slowly transgressed, steadily filling each precious drop of fluid. I could tell that Trina was extremely worried for me.

"I can't believe that I just had a heart attack. I mean, what caused it? I'm so confused!" I blurted.

"I don't know what it is, Alex. I'm just so worried for you. Your entire lifestyle needs to change now. No more junk, no more beer, no more alcohol for a while *now*! The doctor is prescribing medicines that you will need to take for approximately a year now, if not more," Trina said with a stern tone.

The following days after I got discharged from the hospital, I felt like I was a nursing baby at daycare. Trina was watching my every move with the utmost vulnerability and precision, making sure that I didn't need anything. It was hard for me to even pick something up without Trina freaking out. She had called Aunt Mary to supervise me while she was away teaching at the school. I felt like a baby. Every task, once mundane, now felt like a monumental endeavor, almost as if I was taking my first baby step into the unfamiliar world. Lots of friends and family came to visit, dropping ample amounts of flowers, cards, and food. I was overwhelmed with care and joy. I mean, there were so many flowers that I could almost open up a flower shop!

After my heart attack, I had a major realization about how God has bestowed me with a new life. I was utterly thankful because I was not sure what would happen if I left Trina and Brandon behind. I refuse to depart this world carrying unresolved conflicts or ill feelings toward anyone or anyone that I personally know. My biggest desire is to depart this world, knowing that I've fostered joy and led every relationship I have with my loved ones with positivity. I want to be just like Aunt Mary. Any arguments or fights I have had in the past, I have decided to let go, burying them deep. This newfound perspective on life has completely transformed my soul for the better. I mean, God has given me everything I want and more. For that, I am very grateful. The thought of leaving this world, carrying negative intentions toward certain individuals, or without apologizing for my actions wrecks my heart. All I want now is the serenity of knowing that every bond I hold close to my heart is filled with understanding, forgiveness, and an abundance of love.

I am eternally grateful that God has bestowed me with another chance in this life, and I have decided that I want to rekindle with Fran and Victor. I want bygones to be bygones, and I believe that if I give them another chance, they will change. I was worried about telling Trina about this, which is why I wanted to discuss this with her first. Trina was just about to put on her favorite classic TV show, called "Downton Abbey," so she and Aunt Mary could watch, have dinner, and relax. So, I thought that I would talk to her regarding this issue.

"Trina, there's something that has been on my mind for a while now, and I wanted to discuss it with you first. Now, don't get mad, but let me know your thoughts," I said.

She placed her wine glass on the coffee table gently and said, "Alright, Alex, what is it?"

"So after my heart attack, I've been thinking that I want to fix things with Fran and Victor since we all used to be so close to each other," I muttered.

Trina took a pause and then said, "Look, Alex, I get it. Although, I still think you're playing with fire."

"But Trina, I know my boundaries now. And I know what to do and what not to do now."

"Alright, but please keep your distance as well. Not having them over 24/7," Trina spoke firmly, with a tone that carried seriousness.

I spent the following months at home, resting until I was properly able to get back up on my feet. I decided to invite Victor and Fran over to our house for dinner. I told Trina to take me to the nearest Trader Joe's so we could get all the supplies and groceries we needed for dinner. Trina and I decided to throw a taco night, followed by drinks later next to the fire pit. Obviously, I wasn't going to drink, as per Trina's strict orders, and I would have to oblige.

Trina and I went to Trader Joe's and got all the groceries we needed, from all the sauces to canned beans, and we did not hold back. I had been craving tacos for the longest time, and the doctor finally gave me a heads-up to enjoy all the foods I wanted as long as I had a balanced diet.

Victor and Fran arrived at our place at quarter to seven with a gift basket in their hands. I have to admit, seeing them after a while hit me differently. Although they brought somebody else with them, who I didn't know of earlier.

"Hey guys, long time," Trina said.

"Trina, it's so good to see you again. Yes, it has been a while!" Victor said.

It was almost like they, too, had this sudden realization that whatever they were up to just didn't sit right. The first thing Victor said to me was, "Hey buddy, I heard the news about you having a heart attack, and my first instinct was to call you and check up on you. However, due to the circumstances, I wasn't so sure if you would have picked up my call." Victor said in such a heartfelt and genuine way.

"Yeah, like Victor said, it was tragic that this happened. I was about to drop by," Fran said. Don't get me wrong, it was so awkward having this conversation in person.

"Guys, let bygones be bygones. Alex really missed having you guys around, and I missed you guys, too," Trina replied.

"Well, I'm so glad!!" Victor said.

"Let me introduce you to Victor's girlfriend, Michelle; she's from Los Angeles and recently just moved to this town."

Michelle practically shouted *LA* without having to utter another word, flaunting it from her ALO baseball cap right down to the Stanley Cup that she carried, broadcasting her Los Angeles roots loudly.

She seemed sort of young to me, possibly in her late 30s, effortlessly chic and glued to Victor like he's the latest fashion trend. She carried a strict yet intriguing demeanor and seemed super confident.

"Hi! I'm Trina, Alex's wife. It's so nice to meet you! How do you like our small town?" Trina said with a big smile on her face.

"Hiyaa! I've heard so much about you already! Likewise, I honestly loved it because LA was getting too much for me. You know, I'm kind of burnt out. And I'm really glad to have met Victor, who has been a great help showing me around," Michelle retorted in a super cheerful voice.

"Yeah, honestly, it's a treat to live around here. The best place to grow a family and grow old. Like a man just like me," I added. Everyone let out a chuckle and laughed.

"Yeah, Victor told me about your heart attack.

I hope you're recovering alright."

"Well, thank you. Yeah, I'm recovering just fine. Trina's been a great help, and she's not allowing me to eat anything!"

The dinner was a blast; it was good to sit down with old friends once again. We filled Michelle in with all the funny shenanigans that Victor and I had witnessed. It was great fun. I believe that Trina and Fran also solved things and were back to being the great friends they were before this, too. I decided to ask Victor if it was fine if I parked my RV inside his vineyard.

"Of course, buddy. What kind of question is that? I have plenty of space."

His response was great and did not at all imply that he didn't want to have it parked at his vineyard. Since he has five acres of empty land right next to it.

Chapter Six — The Downfall

After the reunion dinner with Fran, Victor, and Michelle, we got close to each other. Especially Trina, Victor, Michelle, and me. They would always come over for dinner, or we would go to theirs. Mostly, on nights out, when we felt young and reckless, we would go to a few pubs and clubs. Our connection with Victor and his girlfriend deepened significantly, evolving to where our daily meetings became a cherished part of our routine. The bond that we shared with them grew stronger, weaving a tight friendship and fostering moments of shared laughter, support, and companionship. I believe that Michelle and Victor are very serious and will get married because he takes amazing care of her. I haven't seen Victor this happy in a while, and he seems like Michelle is the one. Despite Michelle being a lot younger than Victor, they seem like a very compatible couple.

During the summer of 2022, the real estate market was flourishing, and Trina and I found ourselves contemplating a significant life change. We wanted to permanently relocate to Florida since the thriving market and promising opportunities prompted our decision to pursue this major move. We thought it would be great for baby Brandon to move and start school there, too, since there's much more exposure and opportunities in Florida. As I slowly approached my retirement, the perspective of continuing my life in California seemed boring and mundane. Trina and I decided to move and sell our home in California. This was the biggest move Trina and I made since we have never really lived anywhere else other than in Northern California. Our last resort, if things were supposed to go south, was to have the luxurious RV as a backup since it was one great investment that was practically like a home.

Trina and I decided to put our house on a short-term lease for a year, and then we decided that if things were going amazingly well in Florida, we would sell the house forever and keep the huge profits. Since our house is in a great residential area, it can be a great investment for families and couples who prefer to stay in a gated community. The residential area that we reside in fosters a sense of community that embodies one of the finest neighborhoods in Northern California.

I recall June of 2022 being our last month in California, and the saddest part about it was saying bye to Aunt Mary. Aunt Mary is so old that I often worry about her. She prefers living alone since her husband, Max, passed away when she was just 55. Since then, her children have always preferred living out of the country, and Aunt Mary lives alone. During the hot summer months, a dangerously scary and menacing wildfire erupted in our neighboring forest. The ferocity of the blaze brought it concerningly close to our home, suffocating us with the haze of smoke and ash. Stepping out and doing our day-to-day chores was a tedious task, where breathing became an ultimate blessing. The acrid scent of burning wood that kept filling our lungs heightened our risks to life. I was extremely worried for baby Brandon since this is very fatal for a baby. During the entire process of moving, the wildfires that kept erupting gave me utter confidence in taking the huge decision to move my family to another city.

By July 2022, Trina and I finally took the plunge and decided to move to Florida. We decided to stay at one of the rentals that we had bought with the lottery money, which was a duplex in an amazing building. I took a step into this stunning duplex apartment that overlooks the coast and has me by the breathtaking view. This building, called *Casa Nueva,* was a towered glass building with large windows that allowed natural sunlight to flood in and gleam against the polished marbled floors. The modern and urbanized building consisted of cozy furnishing, with contemporary and hip-hop art embellished on each floor. Our new home had three bedrooms, two baths, and a small kitchen. The main lounge consisted of a comfy yet inviting couch that was a snug sofa, so comfortable that I could easily transform into a couch potato any time I wanted!

What Trina loved about this duplex was that she could have her own space once our main unit got a little hectic. Trina decided to turn the other part of our apartment into a sunroom with lots of plants and greenery because that was one thing she didn't want to leave behind in California. She put in a lot of effort and turned a plain living space into a sunroom adorned with an array of different plants and luscious greenery. Her botanical sanctuary was sort of like a safe space for her, and she wanted Brandon to have a room that he could spend most of his time in. She installed a large full-grain leathered couch, which was durable for the sunroom in case of any mishaps. Then she went to IKEA to buy wooded furniture in a light brown color that could match the interior and bring the sunroom together. To elevate the room's entire interior, I hired an experienced painter to paint the wall adjacent to the larger windows. It is a beautiful color with hues of mint and pistachio, embellished with large, intricate flowers. What I loved about this building was that it wasn't too high- tech or excessive; it was the right amount of contemporary and chic. It was a residential building with some really cool people living in it. I was excited about my future endeavors and my retirement because everything here looked magical.

Three months into moving to Florida, Trina and I felt the utmost peace and comfort. I was so grateful to say we were extremely happy with our decision to move here. We finally put Brandon into preschool at a very prestigious school since we wanted no compromises on his education. Brandon had to wear those cute fancy coats as a uniform every time he had to go to school, which made him look like a teddy bear. His school was a 15-minute drive from our apartment, and it was always my duty to pick up and drop him to school. Trina, on the other hand, made Florida into her home pretty fast; she joined a few community groups to make new friends and acquaintances, which never consisted of her family or small-town neighborhood friends that she never really got along with back home. She met lots of like- minded individuals who thought and related to whatever it was she was going through. Trina also applied for a few jobs and got a job that paid her exceptionally well. Since she had a Master's degree in Literature, she got a job at a popular digital agency that hired her as an editorial assistant. It was a very hands-on job since she had to go to work at nine in the morning and return at almost quarter to six. Man, I'm not sure how she did that, but Trina seemed to love it. She would always come back home and tell me all about her work endeavors and the exciting drama that took place at the workplace.

I, on the other hand, found myself quite overwhelmed with my new shift and routine, which felt a bit surreal and hazy at times. Don't get me wrong, I loved my life in Florida, although California will always be home. I mean, I have never lived anywhere else in the world; even the college that I went to was right across town, and I have never left my hometown ever. At times, I really do miss it because the friends that I have back home are like any other. It's hard for an individual like me, who is so introverted and shy, to make friends in such a fast- paced environment in Florida. I miss my fellow officers, my favorite townhouse coffee, my favorite diner, and the beautiful little community to which I devoted my entire life before.

Approximately three months later, when Trina and I made South Florida our new home, I got a call from back home that Aunt Mary had passed away. I remember the exact moment within a flash. It was six in the morning when her son, Hal, called me from Rio de Janeiro, where he had gone for a journalist column. He called me from a random number, and I remember his deep, shaky voice to this day. He said, "Uncle Alex, my mom is gone."

Hal was fighting every inch of grief and shock on that phone call, choking out these words to me with the weight of disbelief and sorrow strained in his voice. I could tell that he tried his best to hold back his tears. In that gut-wrenching moment over the phone, my torrent of emotions got the best of me. I burst into tears as well because if there was one person that I could rely on for dear life, it was Aunt Mary. She has been there with me through all stages of life. She was that one person who never judged me nor was ever stingy toward me. She had the best charisma and strong demeanor that could elevate any room that she walked into. Whether through her sassy, poised gestures, confident stride, or the genuine interest that she took in others, she had the uncanny ability to infuse and radiate any place.

Aunt Mary was a gem of a person, and she loved Trina and me dearly. When I got married, she was the one person who Trina got along with instantly. Aunt Mary was a human form of a teddy bear that would sit with you for hours on end and talk to you about anything that there is. I got out of bed that moment, and Trina also woke up that instant.

"Alex? What's the matter? Are you alright?" she asked while turning on the lamp. She could hear me constantly sniffling and trying to hold back my tears.

"Aunt Mary…" I cried. Tears welled up in my eyes and streamed down my cheeks. This level of sorrow was so unexpected and unprecedented that I was shocked at how this was happening. I had never shed tears like for anyone, not even my own father.

"Oh my… I am out of words," Trina whispered. She came up to give me a very wholesome hug that my body yearned for at the time.

"Trina, the funeral is the day after. And we should go to pay our respects. Will you be able to get off work?" I asked.

"Of course, Alex! How is that even a question? No questions asked, we are going. It's Aunt Mary, for crying out loud! She was so dear to me and close to my heart," Trina was in tears.

The first thing that came to my mind was to call Victor and tell him that we were coming back since I needed the RV ready. Victor insisted that we stay at his house since he felt weird knowing that my family would stay in an RV for the time being. It was very sweet of him to offer us his home to us, and I happily accepted. We left for home the next morning. It was a whirlwind of emotions, and I was left completely numb. The flight from Florida felt like an eternity. The day we arrived back home felt surreal in a strange way. It's not like I was coming back home after ten years or something, although everything felt extremely peculiar. Only this time were we unable to stay at our house since our house was up for lease.

We arrived at Victor's place, and he had two bedrooms, the ones downstairs all prepared for us. Michelle welcomed us with high spirits and a big smile. She was very accommodating and understood that Trina and I needed our utmost space. Victor and Michelle both had dinner prepared for us and made sure that we felt their house was a home for us. The next morning was the day I dreaded the most. It was putting Aunt Mary to rest, and this was the last time I was ever going to see her sweet, warm self. I told Hal and Patrick, her sons, that I was going to cover the funeral costs since I felt like I was obliged to do that. And Trina and I really wanted to. Trina made sure that the funeral arrangements were perfectly done, with beautiful floral arrangements and white roses embossed everywhere. Aunt Mary cherished white roses the most, which is why we made sure they were there at her funeral.

Aunt Mary's funeral was a beautiful and bereaved ceremony. The entire community came to her funeral, even those that she had only briefly met. Her funeral was the epitome of how much people loved and adored her. Her sons, Hal and Patrick, were in utter disbelief and shock, so her passing hadn't struck them yet. It wasn't just a ceremony; it was a heartfelt mosaic of memories, shared stories, and a celebration of her impactful presence and love. Each eulogy given by her senior friends and her sons depicted a perfect portrait of her kindness, her humor, and her crazy anger. After the speeches came to an end, Trina asked everyone if it was alright if I could also share a few words. I was not prepared for this moment; it was automatically sprung upon me. Therefore, whatever that could come to my mind, I said.

I remember my speech to this day so well. I said,

"Aunt Mary. Just her name itself, let alone her presence, could put me in a good mood. To me, she was like another mother. Somebody who took care of me when my parents departed. She was the one who made sure I was alright throughout normal times in life. She was the one who would call me up at night just because she was bored. She was the one who would come over at ungodly hours to share a glass of wine. Not only that, but Aunt Mary shaped me into the man I am today. Her strong demeanor and kindness toward others spoke a thousand words. She made sure to treat anyone who met her with the utmost gentleness and kindness, and that is something that has stuck with me for life. She taught me how to love, how to tackle certain things in life, and most of all, how to be kind to this world. She always used to tell me that this earth that God has gifted us is something we should take care of. We need to be kind to others but also to this planet. She always used to say, 'Alex, we're not here for a long time, but it's a good time.' Everyone in the crowd chuckled. You all know her as the kind grandma who would yank anyone who is misbehaving, although she was the warmest soul out there. She was the sweetest to my son Brandon and my wife Trina, and she always wanted to know how we were doing.

You see, everyone, time is flying by so fast, and we often get busy in our own lives. Although it is so important to take care of our elderly, I urge you all to hug your parents, siblings, friends, and extended family a little tighter tonight. Because if I could hug Aunt Mary just once more, I would. Ahh, and you all know how generous she was after her husband passed. Aunt Mary made sure to give back to the community, as well as feed any hungry mouth there was. And don't get me wrong, she would spoil my family and me rotten! Although, now that she's gone, I just want her to know one thing, and that is Aunt Mary: I will take the best care of your children and will never let them be sad or grieving. You, just rest easy. Your legacy will go on and on for many generations. I love you, legend."

Toward the end, everyone, including myself, was weeping. Victor and Michelle were sobbing at the back, and I was so glad that Trina pushed me to say a few words because it made me feel a little lighter. I was so glad that I got to share my feelings with the community because I really wanted everyone to know Aunt Mary the way I did. Even though they will never have the honor to. After the funeral ceremony ended, we all headed back to Aunt Mary's house for lunch and refreshments. Trina made sure that the food at her funeral was top-notch, so she hired a great catering service to cater the entire event. Her lawyer was present amongst us all because he urged all of us to stay and read her will.

After all the guests had left, it was just her immediate family, Trina and I, and Victor and Michelle, who were waiting for us. I told Trina that we should head back since I felt bad for Victor and Michelle to keep waiting for us. As soon as we were heading out, Aunt Mary's lawyer, Mark, insisted that we stay since I was surprisingly mentioned in the will a couple of times. I personally found that quite amusing since I have no intention of taking anything from Aunt Mary. If anything, everything should go to her sons, Patrick and Hal. We went into another room, where the entire family was present, as well as Trina and me.

The lawyer began to speak and list down all the property and goods that belonged to Hal and then all the property, cars, and funds that were gifted from her to Patrick. Then Mark began to say that 39% of Aunt Mary's wealth would be granted to Hal, and the other 39% would be granted to Patrick. Then, after that, Hal questioned the lawyer: who is the other 22% going to? The lawyer continued to say, Trina and Alex. The lawyer's sudden revelation caused an instant shock, utterly widening my eyes in disbelief. I was so confused. I glanced at Trina, and in return, she met my gaze, both of us staring at one another in a perplexed expression. Since we both were so mind- boggled.

"Hey, Mark? Are you sure? I mean, 22% is a lot, considering Aunt Mary's wealth. I refuse. I believe that all of it should go to her sons," I said gently.

"Nope. That's completely fine. It's Mom's wish," Hal replied.

"Hal, I mean, I don't think it's feasible for me to do this. I refuse to..."

Mark interrupted me.

"So this meeting is over, and the cash will be transferred into your accounts in about a week. Thank you."

"I'm sure there's a way around it? I mean, can't you just transfer our amount into Patrick's?" Trina asked.

"It's Mom's wish. I won't take it, Trina. I happily oblige," Patrick insisted.

As soon as the meeting was over, we all got up to leave. And Hal blurted, jokingly, "Consider yourself winning another lottery, my man. You're a rich man!"

I didn't know what to do with this information. I was so shocked and confused. Everyone got back to their chores, so I told Trina that it was our cue to leave. On the car ride back home, Trina and I were completely shocked by what we had just heard.

"I mean, Alex, I'm sure there's a way around this entire thing?" Trina said

"Yeah, I mean, I will consult my lawyer as well.

Although I also do want to grant Aunt Mary's wishes."

"Yeah, I understand. Anything you decide upon is my decision."

"What are you guys talking about?" Michelle chimed into the conversation.

"Oh, it's nothing. It's about the will, and Aunt Mary granted the will under Alex, and he's not sure whether he wants to accept it or not."

The silence in the car ride spoke volumes on end, and I will never be able to forget that.

Chapter Seven — Our Love Life Was in Shambles

The additional bonus that Aunt Mary has left me made me feel all sorts of ways. I wasn't sure how to go about the situation since I refused to believe that I was the right person to inherit her wealth. I was really content as it was with the money Trina and I had left, and there was not even one bone in my body that disagreed. We reached Victor's house, and he insisted that we stay for a couple more days. He actually even got Michelle to convince Trina, so we had no choice but to extend our stay at their home. I rescheduled our tickets for three days later because it was nice to catch up with old family and friends that I hadn't hung out with in a while.

During our extended stay, I expected to see more of Victor and Michelle since they were the ones who were keen on us extending, though the first two days, they were completely missing. It was pretty unusual since Michelle was always home, trying to feed us her delicious home-cooked meals, and Victor, who pretty much does nothing. I recall a very strange encounter with them once they told Trina and me that they were gone visiting Michelle's Auntie in a town nearby. I clearly remember Michelle telling us that she has no family in Northern California and that everyone here is a stranger to her. When they came back from this two-day trip, without mentioning a word to Trina and me, the story did not add up. They told me that they went to Countabee town, which is supposedly freezing at this time of the year, although they packed nothing but T-shirts for their trip. Don't get me wrong, I don't like looking at the wrong in people, although I have always had my suspicions.

Countabee town is approximately 20 miles from here, and I know for a fact that it is freezing. So why didn't they take any coats with them? Or even a windbreaker? At that moment, I got a little suspicious, and I consulted Trina.

"Trina, it's almost 5 degrees up there, and which aunt lives in

Countabee? I have never heard Michelle talk about her, nor did I know that she had any family up in the north?" I questioned.

"Babe, relax. Maybe they just didn't want to tell us about their whereabouts. Maybe they needed some privacy since we are living in their home?" Trina replied.

"Yeah, but then why did they beg us to extend our trip? I mean, it's rude if you have guests over, and you suddenly dip."

"Yeah, it is pretty unusual, though we can't even be irritated or annoyed since we are living in their house!!" Trina replied in a high-pitched tone.

"Maybe I'm just overthinking and letting it get to my head."

"Hmm, just enjoy, and then we are leaving so soon. Let's not ruin our last few days in our hometown."

I completely brushed off the fact that I found that super off, although I wanted to know if Trina and I were on the same page. She disregarded my overthinking, which made me feel better. The following day was our second last day living with Victor and Michelle. Michelle specifically asked everyone to be at the dinner table by 9 o'clock since we were having a Thai food extravaganza. She specifically told us before that she was cooking all the dishes herself and that we just needed to be there on time. She also told us to wear our best clothes, since it is a fancy dinner, and that we need to wear our best fits to the dinner table downstairs.

At quarter to 9, while I was getting ready, Trina put on the most stunning black dress and did her hair very nicely. She wore a body-con black dress draped amazingly around her brittle body. Trina paired it with some red chunky heels because she knows that red is my favorite color. It was as if I was falling in love with her all over again; it reminded me of the days when we were young and carefree. I cleaned myself a bit also; I wore a nice sky-blue colored button-down and paired it with Trina's most hated pants of mine of all time, the good old beige pants. Trina and I made our way downstairs, where the table was done up so nicely. Michelle had laid out a beautiful spread with delicious appetizers that we could choose to eat from. The ambiance was serene, and the aroma of the food was taking over the entire room. Michelle had lit five large candles embraced in beautiful crystal vases, which made the dinner table look so elegant. On top of the table stood five large candles, with tiny little placards placed in front of them. It was just the four of us, so for that, this dinner was extremely over the top. However, I really appreciated the sweet gesture.

I was assigned to sit next to Victor and right opposite my beautiful wife, Trina. Victor had just headed out to run some last-minute errands, and Michelle was just heading downstairs after all the hassle she went through for us. Michelle also looked very elegant and beautiful, the perfect match for Victor. However, as soon as we began to sit down, pieces of paper were placed right in front of the dinner set. Surprisingly, the torn-out pieces of paper were only placed in front of my plate and Trina's. I was very confused as to what that was and thought I would ask Victor the second he got back.

Around 9:15, Victor made his way back home with expensive bottles of wine. I could tell that it was expensive wine by the looks of the bottle. He told Michelle to place it on the island and that our server would be serving it to us throughout the night tonight. We all sat around the dinner table, looking dapper as ever. It was our last dinner at their house, and I wanted it to be memorable.

"Looking fresh, Alex! Nice shirt," Victor said.

"Well, thank you, Victor. You're free to borrow it whenever you like!" I replied.

"Ha Ha, I'll definitely take you up on that offer, maybe sometime in Florida for sure."

"Hey Alex, I want to share this family tradition I have, and it's going on for generations with you and Trina. I mean, I believe that we all have gotten pretty close, and it's alright to follow strange rituals like this, though it's you guys!!" Michelle exclaimed cheerfully.

"Happily!! We love following family traditions. I believe that they bring all the good luck and fortune," Trina replied.

"Though, you all are already so fortunate. I don't think you need more…" Victor replied condescendingly.

"Victor! That's not a nice thing to say!" Michelle said while trying to glare into the man's soul.

"I was only joking, Michelle! And they know that!"

"So! Guys, basically, all you have to do is pick

up the piece of paper and chant whatever it is that is written on it," Michelle said in a high-pitched tone.

"What sort of family tradition is that?" I questioned.

"Just something my mom always made us do when we were younger. Now come on, start," Michelle said in a stern way.

"Alright, alright," Trina said.

As Trina and I began to chant the words out, Michelle had a strange grin on her face for God knows what reason. And the gibberish that she made us chant out didn't even make sense. I believe that there were some words in Latin that Trina and I had no knowledge of. I couldn't even understand one word of it, and the strange part is that it was only Trina and I who were chanting this strange paragraph. Victor and Michelle remained silent the entire time we were chanting this.

"Alright, guys! Let me take these chits away so we can eat!!" Michelle said.

She immediately took the papers away from us, went into the kitchen, and got rid of them. It was a little strange that Victor was completely silent and remained silent as all of this was unfolding. We began to eat dinner, and Michelle remained missing for a good ten minutes. I started dinner with the Tom Yom soup, followed by some spicy chili wontons and crispy spring rolls. I was halfway through my dinner when Michelle finally appeared and quietly sat in her assigned seating.

"Where were you, Michelle? You can't let us eat all this alone! While you're the one that took hours preparing!" Trina exclaimed.

"That's too kind, Trina. No, I was just on the phone with my mother.

She was just asking about my whereabouts. You know how mothers are!" Michelle replied.

"Uh-hmm, Of course I do! Hope she is well," Trina said while stuffing another crispy spring roll in her mouth.

The very strange thing about all this was that I spotted Michelle's phone on a tiny coffee table right adjacent to the dinner table. I found that extremely odd because then why would she make up this entire lie about her mom? I'm not sure if I believe her anymore. Apart from that, the dinner was divine. From every dish to appetizers and even the dessert, it was all phenomenal. However, after devouring a meal that three people can easily eat, I realized that Victor and Michelle barely ate any food. It was only Trina and I who were stuffing our faces, which made me question why? It was a dinner where we all were supposed to eat, so why didn't they even eat food?

The next morning, it was time for Trina and I to leave home and fly back to Florida. It was a bittersweet feeling; though we came back for a tragic event, it was extremely heartwarming to rekindle with old family and friends. The morning right before we were leaving for the airport, Trina felt extremely ill, to the point where her entire face turned yellow. The trauma of seeing Trina like that all came rushing back to me. I did not want to see her in that state again. She puked about three times, and some of her pukes even turned red. At first, I thought it was food poisoning, although when I witnessed her frightening puke, I truly got scared. This was an emergency, and I knew that I had to rush her to the hospital.

"Babe, you cannot travel like this at all. I'm going to rush you to the hospital," I said.

"No, Alex, I know what has happened, and I cannot believe it," Trina said while crying.

"What TRINA? WHAT IS IT?" I shouted while panicking. Trina began to sob; she sobbed so loudly that it spread shivers down my spine. I low-key knew that whatever it was that she would say next, I was not ready for at all.

"Alex," she sniffled. I went up to her and placed myself right next to her on the edge of the bed, "I've had a miscarriage." As soon as Trina uttered these words, it felt as if all hell broke loose. It felt as if the ground beneath me was opening up to grapple me right in. I began to sweat, and my heartbeat began to expedite.

"What? You were pregnant? You didn't even tell me, Trina." A stream of tears came rushing down my face, where I felt a whirlwind of emotions. "How

could you hide this from me? Trina… I can't believe you hid this from me. And I am so very sorry…"

"Yeah, I… I was waiting to tell you, and then so much ended up happening. All of a sudden, Aunt Mary passed, and I thought I'd wait till we get back to Florida and break you the news," Trina was shaking at this point. "I wanted baby Brandon to have a sibling so bad," she wept.

"Oh my gosh. Trina, I am so very sorry. I am out of words," I gave her one of the tightest hugs ever. Just to make sure that she knows that I am here for her through it all. "Believe me, everything will be fine. I am so so sorry, and I know how much you want another baby," I let my emotions get the best of me, and I began to cry as well.

"How could this happen to me? I made sure to take extra care and precautions so that nothing goes wrong with this pregnancy, so I don't know what happened."

"Trina, baby, don't worry. All will be fine."

"Okay, but don't let anyone know. I don't want a pity party all over again. And, let's head out, we're getting late for our flight," she said.

"What? You're going to go like this? How are you not in heaps of pain? I'm not letting you travel like this," I questioned.

"No, Alex, I just want to get home and cry in my own bed. I can't stay here a second longer. And what's done is done!"

I am unable to understand what had taken place. How could I be so lost and completely miss the fact that Trina was pregnant? And why didn't she tell me? I couldn't even imagine how she was feeling right now. All I knew was that I just had to be there for her and nothing else. As soon as I heard about this traumatic tragedy, I could feel my blood pressure significantly decline, and my arms and shoulders felt insanely heavy to the point where I believed that I was going to fall at any given moment. Though I knew that I couldn't grapple with tensions in front of Trina right now, she was going through so much as it was. I gave it my all to fight my low blood pressure and retort back to reality.

I'm not sure how Trina and I made it back home to Florida that night. There was so much that happened that both of us felt extremely overwhelmed by the turn of events. I just couldn't get over the fact that Trina was pregnant, and now she had had a miscarriage. Our plane ride back home consisted of the worst thoughts ever; it was a whirlwind of the most heart-wrenching thoughts ever. First, it was Trina's miscarriage, Aunt Mary's demise, and then my health conditions; it all felt like a storm of despair. There was so much going wrong that I wasn't sure about what to do. Trina had just lost a child, and watching her sit on the plane near the window seat shattered my heart into a million pieces. She was almost shaking; she sat there staring outside the window, where streams of tears poured down her face. I felt utterly lost, not knowing how to navigate through so much pain and uncertainty. I kept wanting to tell her that it was alright and that everything happens for a reason, though I was scared of saying that because that might have been the last thing she wanted to hear. This entire situation was out of my hands, and I didn't know what to do anymore. Thinking about what my wife was going through was putting me under heaps of tension.

We reached home after a long and miserable journey; even the plane's turbulence questioned our luck. Traveling back to Florida felt like we were moving mountains, trying to get from one place to another. Resuming back to our normal routine felt so confusing and disgusting because it's something every adult HAS to do at the end of the day. Trina wasn't communicating with me right, and she preferred dealing with her emotions on her own. However, I was worried that if she didn't talk about her feelings, she would go on to do something worse. I was worried sick for her. So, I decided to approach her while she was in the midst of changing the sheets in our bedroom.

"Trina, darling. I just want to know how you're holding up with all this. You have barely said anything since we got back. I'm worried for you. Please talk to me," I said in a gentle tone.

Trina scrunched up the bedsheet in a ball and yanked it across the room.

"UGHHHHHHH, LEAVE ME ALONE," she raised her voice. "YOU HAVE BEEN NOTHING BUT IGNORANT ABOUT MY ENTIRE SITUATION. I KNEW SOMETHING LIKE THIS WOULD HAPPEN," she shouted again.

"Excuse me? Trina, you didn't even tell me! How was I supposed to know that you're going through all this? I have also been grieving, just like you are!" I said in a gentle tone.

"EXACTLY. YOU NEVER KNOW ANYTHING. YOU'RE SO CLUELESS, ALEX. AFTER OUR MOVE, WHEN HAVE YOU EVEN THOUGHT ABOUT ME? JUGGLING THIS JOB, KIDS? HOW AM I SUPPOSED TO MANAGE ALL THIS?" she shouted while tears streaming down her face.

"Trina, you're not being fair. And about Brandon... I have been nothing but a great father to him. My aunt just passed, the one that was like a *mother* to me, so all this is extremely unusual for me also."

"And now..." she sniffled again. She collapsed to the floor, consumed by the sobs that seemed to take over her emotions. Each breath became a struggle amidst her uncontrollable crying. Her face is swollen, and her nose turned red, a true testament to the depth of her sorrows and anguish. "I lost another angel in my tummy; I tried for another baby for SO LONG. One wish that I badly wanted to come true has been taken away from me," she cried.

"Trina, we're going to get through this together. I am with you at every step of the way. I apologize if I didn't catch on to you being pregnant, though it will never happen again. Plus, we can try again if you want. Don't worry!" I consoled her. I sat down right beside her and leaned in for a hug.

"Leave me alone, Alex; you don't know what you're talking about.

TRY AS IN HOW? I'M OLD AS IT IS. IT'S TWICE AS HARD," she grappled her arms and wrapped them around her body. Initiating that she didn't want to be consoled. "Leave me the **** ALONE!"

Trina's behavior really shocked me; her loud outburst had me extremely confused and shocked. To the point where I began to contemplate whether or not it was because of me. Was I the reason? No. What did I do? I was out of words. My wife had never been like this, let alone blame me for everything that has gone wrong in our lives. That exact moment shattered all the familiarity I had with Trina. The way she was, to her demeanor toward me, had always been steadfast and supportive, though now has crumbled beneath the weight of pain and blame. Her blame for all the hardships we were going through was directly aimed at me. It was almost as if a storm had swept through our lives, reshaping and messing up the very foundation of our relationship. The relationship that Trina and I had had never been as bad as it was at that point.

Trina decided to crash into Brandon's room, leaving him asleep right next to me; she refused to speak to me, which left my heart in constant worry. I was also extremely angry at her, though what was the reason to fight about all this?

Chapter Eight — The Debacle

It had been a week after that shitshow that Trina pulled, and we hadn't communicated with one another since. This is the longest we have gone since not talking to each other. Every time I would talk to her about reconciling or fixing things, she would burst out of anger all over again, say negative things to me, and then later act as if nothing had happened. I am also a human; I have feelings, too, and Trina should realize that. She took a break from work since it was getting a little overwhelming for her to juggle all this. Therefore, we both were stuck in the house for two weeks without having to speak to one another, constantly being petty and rude to one another. Every day, I would wake up in our room, thinking, "Alright, today is the last day of our fighting." But she disrupts my mood even more and puts me in a worse mood.

I was not sure as to what Trina wanted anymore. It's like even if I breathed in the same

vicinity as her, she would start passing comments and start shouting at me. I mean, I understood that she was going through a lot, but it was no reason to hate your husband or degrade him the second you lay eyes on him. One day, I could recall waking up around 10 am in our master bedroom, with Brandon sleeping right beside me. It was a rainy Saturday morning, and the sun was hidden behind a bunch of clouds, leaving a weathering and weary temperature outdoors. I assumed that Trina would be up and getting ready to go to work, brewing up some coffee, though she was still fast asleep.

I got up from my bed to check up on her, and the alley to Brandon's room was dimly lit. The lamp on the table was still turned on, which meant that Trina hadn't come out of the room. I slowly began to open the door, and Trina was fast asleep with her hands wrapped tightly around Brandon's favorite stuffed toy, an animated giraffe with soft and fluffy fur. It was Brandon's favorite stuffed toy since it was his constant companion. It was filled with vibrant colors and textures. I walked into Brandon's room and turned the lamp off; I kept slowly taking Trina's name for her to wake up. After the fourth attempt to rouse her, I began to get a little concerned as to why Trina wasn't waking up. Her lack of response raised alarming questions and a growing sense of unease.

"Trina! Baby, wake up." I gently shook her, hoping she was merely lost in a dreamlike haze. However, despite my efforts, she remained lying there, unresponsive, in a deep unconsciousness. I panicked and called 911 immediately. I immediately checked her pulse and thanked the LORD for it was still running. I let out a huge sigh of relief and patiently waited for the ambulance to come to my rescue. Watching Trina in that state gave me shocks that I had only gotten over the last time she was in the hospital. Especially since I haven't spoken to her for the past few weeks of our fighting.

The ambulance took exactly nine minutes to come, which gave me plenty of time to change Brandon's clothes and call his babysitter, who luckily lives in our building. Teara arrived instantly when I told her that I had to rush Trina to the hospital. I packed Trina a bag of all her essentials and immediately left for the hospital. As soon as I saw the two nurses put her brittle body on the stretcher, tears came pouring down my face. I was unable to fathom losing my wife, especially after Aunt Mary. The worst thoughts came into my mind, like what Brandon and I would do without Trina. How will I lead my life like this now? All alone? How will I grow old without having Trina by my side? The loneliness will ultimately kill me!! However, I knew that I needed to put emotions aside and take matters into my own hands right now.

On our way to the hospital, I sat in the front seat with the kind driver who was driving us there. He told me to stay calm and not to panic. Through all this, I turned around to see Trina being wrapped in a blanket, and the nurse readied the automated defibrillator, poised to administer a shock to her. The scene unfolded in a flurry of urgency; the other nurse prepared a critical intervention as the gravity of the situation became palpable. I opened the tiny window and shouted, "WHAT IS HAPPENING TO MY WIFE?"

To which they replied saying, "Sir, we would advise you to stay calm in this situation and not panic. We are doing our best to treat your wife and will reach the hospital shortly."

"ALRIGHT, BUT WHAT CAUSED THIS? SHE WAS PERFECTLY ALRIGHT LAST NIGHT," I questioned.

"From the looks of it, your wife has a vascular disease that has blocked all her blood vessels that carry oxygen throughout the body. Lots of her arteries remain to be blocked. For some instances, her body has a very low percentage of hemoglobin, which we are trying to figure out why." The nurse was very patient and understanding and really calmed me down.

"She's going to be alright, though, right? Also, I believe that she has lost lots of amount of blood because she had a miscarriage two weeks ago," I said.

"Oh, I'm so sorry. We will look right into it."

We reached the hospital in exactly six minutes, and Trina was rushed into the ER. I patiently waited outside and waited for the doctor to tell me what was up. Her surgery took about three and a half hours, and then the doctor came outside to tell me.

"Hi, you must be her spouse?" he said.

"Yes, I'm Alex. What happened to her, Doc?

"Well, Trina's situation right now is a little critical; she just went through vascular surgery, commonly known as open surgery, where I treated her aortic aneurysms, peripheral arteries, and her carotid artery as well," he said politely.

"Wow. Okay, though, what caused this?"

"Well, it varies from patient to patient, although I believe that one of her arteries that is connected to her brain stopped functioning, which is why she was unable to respond or even move."

"Did the surgery go well?" I hesitated to ask.

"The best it can go, honestly. Though I'm not sure what exactly caused this. I was looking at her past medical records, but there's nothing as such that is so alarming. Are there any irregular habits that your wife has picked up? Like smoking or maybe even a new gym routine?" he asked.

"No? As you may know by now, my wife had a miscarriage about two weeks ago. And it was very traumatic for her. She refused to eat proper meals and would often skip them. Can that be more of a reason?"

"Nope, women go through miscarriages all the time. Though it was extremely heartbreaking, their bodies can go back to normal by eating just two Panadols. So I'm not sure where this illness has sprung up from," the doctor said.

It was quarter to 4, and Trina had finally woke up from her sleep. She was under anesthesia, so it was a task to wake her up again. Upon my trying to wake her up, the only words that came out of her mouth were, "Alex, please come and find me" or "Alex, is Brandon okay?" in a fuzzy voice. She started humming a random song that I had no recollection of and asked me to join in. I was glad that she woke up in a great spirit and that all the fighting and arguing that we had been doing for the past two weeks were left in the books.

"Trina baby, are you alright? I am worried sick."

"Thank you, Alex, I'm so grateful. What happened, though?" Trina asked in a high-pitched tone.

"You weren't waking up, baby. You weren't responding, which is why I freaked out and rushed you to the hospital," I said.

"OH! Well, here I am! Did the doctors say anything?" she said in a chirpy mood.

"Well, they told me that you have a vascular disease and that you will need to take medication for the rest of your life for it. It's pretty critical, Trina."

"What? I had no idea. Is it curable?"

"Unfortunately not. We just need to take proper care of you now. More than ever. I don't know what will happen to me if anything happens to you," I said, knowing that my voice was cracking.

"Alex, stop. I'm not going anywhere. Though, it means that I can definitely not have any more kids," she said.

"Trina! That's the last thing that is on my mind right now. All I care about right now is your health, and thank god you're fine now!" I said.

"Excuse me? So what you're trying to say is that you don't care about having another child? Right.

I see how it is," her tone switched up so fast that I was confused.

"No, I didn't mean that. All I meant was that you get fine for now. Geez."

"Yeah. Right."

I had automatically assumed that Trina would be over that entire debacle, although it did not seem very likely. During the days of having her back home, I made sure to be the best husband by being there for her through anything that she needed. I made sure to give her medication on time, to put her favorite show on for her every night, and to even order her the healthiest meals. I made sure to make the bed every morning and make her favorite cup of coffee. Although, for some reason, all of this never seemed enough.

Trina's frequent outbursts seemed to escalate, becoming increasingly irrational and unpredictable. She would start shouting and erupt over the randomest matters. She would fight with me for putting the cup down in a certain way or even, at times, over Brandon. She shouted at me for treating him the way I was or not being able to give him his food on time. It was getting so overwhelming to the point where even if I breathed in front of her, she would have a problem with it. The tension reached a breaking point where even the simplest actions I took seemed to invite her ire. Living in that period felt like an emotional whirlwind, leaving me feeling as though walking on eggshells was the only way to navigate our interactions.

I'm not sure what Trina was going through, though it was definitely emotions of hate toward me. Despite her illness, I didn't have the heart to argue with her or fight. I was always scared of losing her to another unannounced attack.

Two months later, when Trina had properly recovered and was back up on her feet, she resumed her office. She began going on these long shifts, leaving Brandon and me home all alone during most of our time.

I wasn't sure what to do with my time. I felt lonely. Therefore, I decided to have a conversation with her. I shared all my concerns. And the only response I got after that was, "Alex, I'm not sure what you want from me. I am recovered and healing, yet you have complaints."

"Trina. You know it's not about that. You just haven't been yourself lately, and it hurts me to know that."

I didn't know what I had exactly done to deserve this treatment from my wife. Home didn't feel like home anymore, and we were fighting like cats and dogs. At one point, I believed that Trina hated my existence; she made me feel so useless and worthless at times just because I was retired. Just because I was lazying up at home, I mean, I told her that it was time to retire, and she had no problem with it. In fact, she even told me that it would be a great idea if I retired since we would get more time to spend with one another and give time to Brandon. Although, now I believe that I only have a better understanding and friendship with my baby boy.

The following morning, it was time for our monthly grocery run, and it was high time that we stocked up on our groceries. I asked Trina if she wanted to come along, and she said, "I would rather *rot at home alone.*"

At that point, I lost it, "Do you even hear yourself? What's gotten into you? I am trying my best for us to reconcile, although you're not letting me do ANYTHING! I believe that even if I breathed next to you, you would get irritated. WHAT'S THE MATTER, TRINA?" I hurled.

"LOWER YOUR VOICE RIGHT THIS INSTANT!" she shouted back.

"NO, I WILL NOT! TILL YOU DON'T TELL ME WHAT'S THE MATTER WITH YOU, I WILL NOT!" I replied.

"FOR GOD'S SAKE, ALEX, LOWER YOUR VOICE," she shouted back.

"NO, I WILL NOT!" I was fuming with rage.

"YOU'RE RIGHT! I CAN'T STAND YOU RIGHT NOW; EVERYTHING YOU DO IS MAKING ME WANT TO BANG MY HEAD AGAINST THE WALL. FOR MONTHS, I HAVE BEEN FIGHTING THIS SUDDEN HATRED I HAVE GOTTEN FOR YOU.

EVERYTHING YOU DO REPULSES ME. I LOST A BABY BECAUSE OF YOU! EVERYTHING THAT IS GOING WRONG IS ALL

BECAUSE OF YOU!" Trina was exhilarated and thrilled to have finally blurted these words out.

"EXCUSE ME? BECAUSE OF ME? EVERY DECISION I MAKE IN THIS LIFETIME IS THE DECISION YOU HAVE AGREED TO. SO WHY IS THE BLAME ON ME?" I was furious; I couldn't believe that Trina was blaming me for all that had gone wrong. I mean, how could she?

"Yeah. That's right. You can take Aunt Mary's wealth and shove it up your a**!" Trina replied sarcastically.

"SCREW YOU!" I blurted the second she landed on the floor. Right after that moment, a surge of mixed emotions flooded my brain. I was angry, emotional, and grieving. How could she use Aunt Mary as an excuse? How could my wife stoop so low?

There was this inexplicable surge within me, an intense anger that surpassed any ability to articulate. It felt like a blaze of anger clouded my judgment, engulfing every thought and emotion and leaving me consumed by a tempest of anger. I am unable to put into words how I felt at that exact moment, where it took over my rage and operated through a wavelength of body language. In the wake of that impulsive act, shame and regret collided within me, which created a turbulent mix of emotions. As I stood a foot away from Trina, having just pushed her with an unexpected force, a flood of remorse washed over me. The immediate satisfaction of retaliation swiftly dissolved into a hollow realization of my disgusting actions.

However, I was also utterly ashamed of the fact that this was the first time ever in my life that I laid a hand on my wife. Tears came flooding down my cheeks because I knew that this was an act that only cowards do. Never in my life have I EVER even thought of or dared to lay a hand on a woman like this. I knew that from now on, our entire relationship will change for the worse. I'm not sure what got into me or how I could even let my anger get the best of me.

"OW! Ale…" Trina cried.

When I heard Trina's silent weeping pierced through the air, it weighed heavily on my conscience. Hearing the sounds of her in pain echoed like a haunting symphony of pain as I stood there frozen. Enveloped in a nightmarish reality of my own doings. It was as if I had stumbled into a crime scene, where the killing weapon was clutched tightly in my hands,

staining everything it touched. It was hard for me to catch some air, with the weight of my actions and a sickening sense of disbelief that grappled me. I realized that I had caused this hurt and devastation. My chest tightened with a suffocating sense of guilt and fury. I am not this man and never was. I wanted to go help Trina up, but I was just so angry that I stood there still.

"What is wrong with you, Alex? How can you push me like that? What's happened to us?" she cried; she sniffled her nose, "I can't stay like this any longer. I want to separate for a while, and I'm taking baby Brandon with me." The pain in her voice startled me.

"Yea. Alright, I won't stop you."

"Do you even realize what you have just done? My arms have already started to bruise." As Trina's tears fell, her voice quivered with an unbearable ache, and each word strained through the weight of all that had taken place right now. Amidst her tears, she struggled to form proper sentences, and her voice cracked with the uncertainty of her emotions.

"I'm sorry." I had nothing else to say because the intensity of the entire situation was a lot bigger than me just pushing her. That night, Trina wore a spaghetti-strapped tank top with her favorite Lulu lemon pants, and when I pushed her, I could see her left arm bruised up because she used that arm as support. She reached out with her left arm to steady herself, and I could see a bruise form when she landed. The force of the push made her stumble and crash into the coffee table with a loud bang. She lost her footing and ended up falling right next to the long L-shaped couch when the entire room was filled with sobs.

"I don't know what's happening with me, Alex. And I genuinely apologize for saying that about Aunt Mary. I am so very sorry. I don't know what's happening with me or you," Trina said while crying.

I walked out of the room because I needed to collect my thoughts. I was really overwhelmed with all that was happening. The only person I thought of calling was Trina's father because I was feeling extremely guilty about what I had done. I rang the phone. It was daytime in Vietnam at the time, and he picked up after the phone rang for the third time.

"Hello, Alex! What a surprise. What's the matter? You called so abruptly," he asked. His voice truly put my anxiety aside and calmed me down.

"Hi, I just wanted to talk to you about some things. Trina and I…" and my voice started to crack. "Trina and I have been going through a very rough period. We're constantly fighting, and we can't see eye to eye anymore. What should I do? You're the closest person to me now, other than my wife." My voice carried such deep anguish that it was evident that I was under immense stress.

"What happened? You are worrying me, Alex!" Trina's father sounded extremely worried.

"I just did something that can't be reversed. And Trina and I keep constantly fighting. And then she's also been rushed to the hospital. I don't know which dark cloud is hovering above us, though I really need your prayers." I said.

"My son, Alex you are like my son, worry not!! I believe that Trina and you should take a flight to Vietnam as soon as possible. Please come; my house is open for you guys."

"You know what? Maybe you're right; we should take a trip to Vietnam and figure all this out."

Chapter Nine — The Confrontation

Trina and I haven't spoken about the fight we had because both of us were extremely ashamed of our actions. Since I knew that we weren't going to figure anything out ourselves, it was time to go to Vietnam. I consulted with her before and made sure that she was allowed to go because of her health issues. I booked our tickets for the next flight because my phone call to Trina's dad really worried him. He kept saying that there is an evil black cloud over us and that there is a lot of negative energy that is surrounding us. He said that we needed to get to Vietnam as soon as possible so that we could get cured. Surprisingly, Trina agreed because she also knew that everything that was taking place was not normal.

Our flight to Vietnam was at five in the morning from San Francisco. There were no direct flights that took place, and these were the best plane tickets that I could find at the time. We decided to take *Virgin Atlantic* since they were the cheapest tickets that were being sold, so it was last minute. Since we didn't book a return ticket, we had to take baby Brandon along with us because Grandpa really wanted to see him.

We left for San Francisco at 2 am, and the entire time, Trina was constantly complaining and nagging about how I booked the worst tickets. I also realized that I could've been smarter about booking tickets directly from our airport back home. The entire trip to Vietnam consisted of nagging but also a lot of silence, which was extremely unusual for Trina and me because traveling is our favorite hobby. We usually end up rekindling and talking about random things that we want to accomplish in life while traveling, although it wasn't the same anymore.

Once we got to San Francisco, I believed that all the evil spirits and negative energy would disappear from around us. The weather was extremely nice and chilly, and the city was still booming at 3 in the morning. However, Trina was still in a bad mood, and to be honest, I don't blame her for being in one. We reached San Francisco International Airport, and the energy inside that airport was extremely uplifting and jovial. I had a great feeling about flying to Vietnam, and I had a feeling that whatever it is that is putting Trina and me through these never-ending obstacles will surely suffice. We hoped on the plane to take a direct flight to Ho Chi Minh City, though the flight was about a day long. We were on the plane for about 20 hours, and the flight from California to Ho Chi Minh City felt like an eternity. After eating our second meal on the plane, which was breakfast, at I don't even know which time zone, Trina seemed to be in a chirpy mood. I knew that this was the best time to talk to her since she was two glasses of wine down.

"Hey baby, I know it's taken me about two whole days to say this, but just know that I am so so very sorry for pushing you like that. You know I am a man of honor, and I would *never* do anything to hurt you. And I know that this apology will never suffice for my actions, though I just want you to know from the bottom of my heart that I am sorry. I hope that this doesn't affect our marriage from now on, and I want you to know that you can *always* count on me for you and Brandon. I promise."

"Alex, thank you for this apology and just know that I will need some time to recover from this. What you did hurt me more than you will ever understand. I get it. You're my husband, though you had absolutely no right to do that," Trina exclaimed.

"Trina, you also said some very rude things. I am *also* hurt. Don't get me wrong, I let my anger get the best of me, though let's not act like you're the only one who's innocent here," I said in my defense.

"Yeah, whatever. Alex, you don't even understand the amount of stress I'm going through. *My hair* is falling out. I said what I said. I'm not sure what's happening to me either. I'm going crazy. I have all these intrusive thoughts that I can't seem to fight. I think I'm going crazy, and I don't know what to do about it," Trina said, and I could tell that her voice was about to crack. I looked up to see her face, and she was quivering.

"I know, and I hate to see you like this. Don't worry, everything will be fine soon."

I gave her my arm so that she could lean onto it, making sure that I would always be there.

We reached Ho Chi Ming City after 20 hours of exhaustion and travel. As soon as we landed, we were hit by the city breeze and warmth. People were hurling all over each other the second we got out of the airport, where I could smell the distinct air with an aroma of fish. Since the sea was so close to us, the air was crisp and breezy. I had a good feeling about coming to Vietnam after more than a year. Trina's father was patiently waiting for us, standing next to his worn-out Sudan, ready to welcome us with open arms. The second we approached his car, he jogged toward us and grabbed Brandon into his arms.

"My beautiful boy!!! So good to see you. You've grown up so much!" he said.

He was getting a little teary as he cradled Brandon into his arms. Brandon, the jolly toddler that he is, was extremely happy to be in Grandpa's arms once again. He looked at Trina and me and immediately said, "What's happened to the both of you? I didn't leave you guys like this?"

"What can I say, Papa? There is so much that's happened."

Meanwhile, Trina was lugging her hand carry onto the front seat of the car since our sturdy luggage took all the remaining space at the back of the trunk. She shut the car door behind her and ran toward her father, "Papa!!! I've missed you so much." She threw her arms wide, reaching toward the sky, before wrapping them around her father in a hug so tight, it seemed to gather every bit of love and emotion she could muster, expressing a depth of affection that she'd never before revealed.

"Oh!!! My Con cai!! How I have missed you so much. You have become so brittle. Are you not eating enough? And what is this I'm hearing? You have been fighting with poor Alex?" Trina's father questioned.

"It's a long story, Papa. Let's head home, and I will tell you all about it."

"Yes, you must."

"Also, how did you know that Alex and I have been fighting? Has he said something to you?" Trina asked.

"Hahaha, I might have consulted a few things or two with the old man!" I said sarcastically while landing a high-five with her father.

"Hmm, I'll have a talk with you two once we're home!"

We buckled up in the car and drove home. I rolled down the window to grasp the city air and Ho Chi Ming's bustling cityscape. It felt like stepping into a whirlwind of positive energy and vitality. The streets thrummed with an orchestrated chaos. The type of chaos that I was craving for many days. A symphony of motorbikes assembling from all corners, weaving and flying through traffic. I am not going to lie; the traffic and driving style here get me a little anxious, though every country has its own persona. Their honks tweak seamlessly with the lively chatter of street vendors and the tantalizing aromas wafting from each food stall. The amount of street food that I was planning to have this trip was definitely a little concerning. Creative and neon signs illuminated through miles of distance, casting an inviting yet vibrant glow to the city markets where locals and visitors like us would like to mingle and shop. In this urban town, every sight, sound, and scent coalesces into a sensory overload, offering a thrilling invitation to Vietnam's city life.

After a 45-minute drive from the airport, we reached Trina's childhood home, the same one we stayed in last time. However, this time, the house looked more vibrant and cozy. For the longest time, Trina and I were in and out of apartment buildings, where this house had a cozy and comfortable vibe to it. As I stepped onto the creaky wooden porch, Trina's home stood before me. A freshly painted fawn color on the walls, and I met with a new and sturdy porch swing, which I assumed her father loved to sit on while having a nice cup of tea. The thatched roof stood over our heads, sheltered timeworn stories and tales of generations in the past. The wooden shutters had weathered countless seasons and guarded the old, sturdy windows like loyal sentinels. What I loved about these windows was that they would allow streaks of warm sunlight to filter inside.

The entire vibe of that place was beyond comforting. As you step inside, you're welcomed by the crackling fireplace and the never-ending kitchen. Trina's father was huge on cooking and making home-cooked meals. As soon as we arrived, he had three stoves on, in a lower flame setting, with three dishes cooking up. As I scanned the kitchen, I also saw that he had prepared us even more fresh dishes that were lined up just like a lunch buffet at certain hotels. I was so excited to devour all this mouth-watering food. Trina had gone in to freshen up while I helped her father bring in all the luggage.

"Alex, what's happening with both of you? Tell me everything. You know I have been so concerned for the past week."

"Father, there is so much. I just feel like a bad omen or evil cloud is hovering over us right now. I don't know what it is, and we just never stop fighting. She is just always ready to point all the blame on me."

"I think I might know. There is an old Vietnamese tale that tells us about black magic. And you know, it's so true. Black magic is so common around here, and I believe something like that has happened with you guys," Trina's father was convinced that it was somebody else's doing.

"I mean, I'm not sure, honestly. Because her behavior is so unpredictable. It's constantly like I am walking on eggshells every time we have a conversation. Right after she had her miscarriage, she constantly blamed everything for going wrong because of me. Can you believe it? She said that I was the cause of her miscarriage," I said under a breath.

"Oh my gosh. My child had a miscarriage? And none of you decided to even tell me about it? Is she alright? No wonder why she's become so weak and brittle. Oh my! I am so worried for the both of you." Trina's father put both his hands on his forehead because he was so shocked about all that I had just said.

"What are you guys talking about? Papa, why do you look so shocked? What did I miss?" Trina walked in from the back, wiping her hands off the towel.

"My child, I just found out that you went through a miscarriage. I am so very sorry, my child." He started sobbing, grabbed Trina, and kissed her forehead. His silent quivering could just tell me that he was so hurt by hearing this news. He never wanted to see his daughter suffer so much. It made me emotional.

"Papa, I don't want you to worry now. I am good," Trina finally gave him some assurance to let him know that she was okay.

"I want you to meet this lady that sits two hours away from the city, and she cures evil and controls all the evil spirits and black magic that you might have been surrounded with. I believe that we must pay her a visit since I think some gnarly black magic has been done on you guys."

"Papa, we are already so exhausted, and now you want us to trek two more hours away from the city to meet some woman? Plus, I don't really believe in this black magic business anyway."

"Trina, no, I think we should listen to your father and see what this lady has to say. I mean, it could definitely be knowledgeable, and we can take preventive measures next time. And also, I do agree with him. I think there is most definitely a bad omen that is following us around because since we have moved to Florida, our life has been a roller-coaster."

The father-daughter bond that Trina and her father have is uncanny. It's something that I craved so deeply as a child. I believe that he had taught her how to be an independent and stellar human through all his experiences. People should admire the way Trina's father raised her because the way he had taught her to look for the best in people and treat people right is how I would want every parent to raise their child. I have always admired her courage and strength through difficult times, and she has always been my strongest backbone in times I needed her.

We crashed super early that night since we were extremely jet lagged from our never-ending flight, so we went to bed by 7 pm. Trina's father advised us to be up by 5 am since this lady that we were about to meet only sat for three hours, and that even depended on her mood. So we had to catch this lady fast. I was half asleep on the way to this lady's house while Trina and her papa were blasting music in the front. This random lady's home was on the outskirts of the city, where the landscape shifted dramatically from the bustling city we called home to a sprawling expanse of verdant fields and the rows of crops stretched endlessly across the lands.

I believe that she lived in some village where the vibrant greenery painted a picturesque scene, where each leaf and blade swayed into the breeze. As far as my eyes could see, luscious green hills rolled across the horizon, where my eyes captured patches of colorful wildflowers that added a touch of whimsy.

The air carried the earthly fragrance of the crisp summer air mixed with freshly tilled soil. The scent of sweet scent blossoms and the fields created an intoxicating yet inquisitive smell, which I really appreciated. You don't get to smell the countryside like this back home.

As soon as we reached this lady's house, all I could see was that she lived in a very old and small home. Before entering her premises, we walked through a worn-out cobblestone path, with a tiny little garden nestled on the right corner of the house. I'm assuming that she's a huge fan of gardening since I could see a variety of flowers being grown in her nursery. Toward the left of the entrance stood a nicely custom-painted Land Rover that was in pristine condition. I was a little shocked since Land Rovers are pretty pricey, and by the looks of this lady's house, I didn't think she could afford it.

Trina's father guided the way since he had been there a couple of times. The front porch of this lady's house had chairs spread out, almost in a line for visitors to come and wait. The distinct smell of aged wood and faint traces of sweet, comforting spices were wafting through the air, hinting at all that goes down in this house. As soon as I stepped foot into this home, I felt as if I was being stared at by thousands of people. There was this strange vibe that I couldn't exactly put into words. All of a sudden, I felt very heavy on my shoulders, as if someone was heavily burdening me with negative energy.

We walked into this hollow room, which was dark, with natural sunlight peeking through a cracked window. In front of the old lady lay a large cobblestone bowl, and right beside it were a number of medicines and natural herbs. The lady herself was sitting on the plane concrete ground, engrossed in a thin linen woven fabric wrapped all around her. The lady was so old that the skin all around her pearly white eyes was sagging to her cheeks, surrounded by delicate, sagging skin that held a twinkle of wisdom and warmth that seemed to defy the years. Her face was a map of time that was etched with deep lines and creases that traced stories from a lifetime. Each movement revealed the fragility of her bony frame as if a gentle breeze might indeed threaten to shatter her delicate form. Despite her stature, her presence commanded respect and exuded a quiet strength that spoke volumes of experiences weathered and conquered. She was definitely 90 or more years old, her hair a river of silver cascading down to her back in a meticulous braid, all the way to her hips. In her fragmented aura, her appearance lay a beauty of wisdom that transcended a lifetime of resilience and grace that reflected in every fragile yet resilient facet of her being.

"Chao Mung," the lady announced. "Chao Chao, Ma," Trina's father replied.

"Vậy Tại Sao Hôm Nay Bạn Lại Dến Dây Với Tôi?" she said. I didn't speak Vietnamese, though Trina and her dad were fluent in it. I guess that she asked us why we came.

"Tôi rất lo lắng cho con gái tôi và chồng nó. Họ liên tục gây gổ và gần đây cô cũng bị sẩy thai. Vì vậy, bạn có thể vui lòng cho chúng tôi biết liệu có điềm xấu nào đang cản trở phước lành của họ không?" As Trina's father was conversing, Trina translated everything that he was saying to her. He told the old woman that he is deeply worried for us, and that we constantly keep fighting. He also told her that Trina has had a miscarriage.

The old woman then told Trina and I to come forward and place our hands in her palm. As soon as we did, the old woman had a surprising reaction; her eyes were shut, and it was as if she was looking back at our tragic life events. She took a good two minutes while she clenched our palms, and to be honest, I felt as if I was finally being healed. I'm not sure why I blindly trusted that woman, though I had a feeling that we had come to the right place.

After she was done reading our palms and examining the situation, the old lady opened her eyes in a way that expressed extreme concern and trouble. She gasped and told Trina's father that Trina and I had been in extreme trouble. The old lady began to yell, and to my knowledge, she kept asking Trina's father why he brought us to her so late.

"Why do you bring them to me now? What is done is already done!!" she yelled, and Trina translated, being shocked.

"No, Ma. They live in the United States, so traveling all the way here for them is a little hard."

"Well, the bad omen seems to be following them around constantly for about a year now. Not only a bad

omen but the worst form of black magic has constantly been done on you and your family for years now!!" the lady exclaimed.

"What? Papa, tell her to tell us more."

"Ye. You both won the lottery? Which brought in newfound wealth into your home. It changed your life for good, though there is something extremely bad and horrible that wanted all your blessings to go away. They tried to take everything from you. They didn't even leave your son, Brandon." I could hear the regret and shame in the lady's voice. She sounded extremely concerned.

"Oh my gosh. But who could it be, Ma? Trina and Alex live alone in California, and they have no extended family over there. Plus, nobody but I knew about the lottery winning? Please can you elaborate?" Trina's father said.

"It is not family. I am sorry, but I don't reveal lots of information about who it could possibly be, who did the black magic. However, all I can say is that three individuals are involved in this act..." the lady announced.

As soon as those words left the lady's mouth, a heavy silence enveloped the room. The weight of her words seemed to echo through the core of my being. The realization hit me like a truck, making me question every past decision I may have made in the past year or so. It felt as if all this time, Trina and I had been blinded by whatever it was and ignored the biggest signs. The first two people that I have always had my suspicions about were Fran and Victor. However, after my heart attack, I was the one who extended my arms wide open and let them back into our lives. There was proper evidence on how it could be Fran, and we haven't seen Fran in a while, so it's possible that it could be her. More than anything, I am hurt. I can't believe that our closest friends would do such a vile thing like this. After all this time, I let them into my home and met my beautiful little baby boy, and every time they needed anything, I would be the first to offer any help I could. The collision of disgust and heartbreak created a storm of conflicting emotions that clouded my thoughts constantly at the time.

The lady then said, "But don't you both worry.

I will try my best level to cure this magic so that you all are free from this negativity and toxicity. Though, I cannot do anything about your son, Brandon." As these words left her lips, my heart fragmented into countless shards. I sensed that what she was about to reveal would be a revelation of something so shocking, so horrifying, that neither Trina nor I had any recollection of. My heart was beating.

"What do you mean?" Trina asked anxiously.

"Your son, I think you call him Brandon. He is diagnosed with Leukemia. And it will not be curable," the lady said in such a firm tone. "They have not even left your son alone; whoever these people are, you need to cut them out of your life. They are despicable. They are evil, from all the evil that is out there," the lady added.

"What are you saying, Ma? That cannot be possible…" Trina's father started sobbing so profoundly that the next-door neighbors were able to hear him. Trina was standing at the back end of the little concrete-made room in silence.

"My life is over. This lady just told me that my life is practically over." I believe that Trina was numb because of the shock that she was in; she was unable to comprehend the true gravity of the situation. When I heard those words come out of her mouth, I simply collapsed. I felt as if I was going to have another heart attack at any given moment. I couldn't believe what I had just heard about my son, and I prayed to God to bless me once more and let this not be true now.

Chapter Ten — Vietnam

Having to sit on that cold concrete floor and hear the most bizarre news about Brandon felt as if I had just been shot directly in my heart. Everything around me felt surreal, to the point where I had to pinch myself to see if I was dreaming or not. At that moment, I felt as if my entire respiratory system was being shut down. From each vein to my lungs, it felt like vigorous ropes of anxiety and tension were caging them. I started sweating profoundly and needed fresh air as soon as possible. I didn't want Papa or Trina to see me like this, so I slowly got up and exited the lady's home. I immediately needed to catch my breath because it felt as if I was going to have another heart attack at that moment. I started coughing like a mad dog, trying to keep my blood sugar levels up, and slowly paced toward the car. I make sure that every time I leave the house, I tell Trina to keep my medicine bag, just in case of an emergency. I got to the car, and thankfully, it wasn't locked. I instantly opened the front door and reached for Trina's bag. Hoping to God that she kept my medicine bag in this bag of hers.

Thankfully, I found my medicine bag and reached for the aspirin. At that point, I felt the pain slowly reaching the back of my shoulders and gradually increasing toward my jaw. I was shaking. I couldn't create a scene because I knew that this was not the time or place, and nor was that the time to ask Trina to come to help me since she was going through an awful time herself. I plucked the aspirin out of its packet as fast as I could and swallowed it as if my life depended on that one pill. I crumbled and sat against the car door on the ground. There was nothing around me but fields of green crops surrounding me. It was so quiet that I could feel my own heart beating so loudly and a few birds chirping on neighboring trees. I was so overwhelmed with what I had just heard that I broke down. Tears came rushing down my face like they had never before. I was crying and whimpering so much that only God could hear my pain. I profoundly cried, to the point where I was unable to stop. I couldn't get a hold of myself. Hiccups followed, and they were so loud that it sounded like a big baby was whimpering.

I sat there on the muddy floor, with my back against Trina's father's rusty car, and I held my hands together and prayed to God. I said, "I know I never reach out to you. I know I am not religious, and you probably think that I am only reaching out to you now because the situation has gotten so bad. Though yes, it has, God. I pray you forgive me. I pray that you take all of Trina and Brandon's sadness and grief and give it to me." I cried so much, and I knew that this was the time when I hit rock bottom. "Give it to me, my lord. If winning the lottery and having this much wealth wins you this, then take it all back. I don't want it. TAKE IT BACK!!! I just want my family to be okay. We were perfectly fine before this. So please take it back. Let my family be happy again."

I felt extremely better after I confided with God. I got a hold of my emotions, and it felt as if the pain that was on my shoulders was lifting off. I reached to take a tissue out of my pocket, wiped my nose, and decided to enter the lady's home again.

As soon as I entered the room, Trina was a mess. It was as if someone had told her that she would never be able to see Brandon again. Papa, on the other hand, was on his knees, hugging Trina so tightly and comforting her, saying, "It's okay, my love. Everything will be alright. We have come to this lady for a reason. Don't you worry, my child? Be strong."

"Where were you, Alex?" Trina sniffled.

"I just went out to eat an aspirin. My chest felt extremely tight after hearing this news, and I needed fresh air."

"Oh no, Mija!! Are you okay?" Papa asked. "Yes, I'm okay."

I sat down right in front of the lady, and she was waiting for us to get done with the emotional wrecks we were in so she could proceed with the procedure, "I am sorry for breaking the news to you about your baby boy so insensitively. I can see that he is very loved. Although, there is so much evil around you both that it is starting to scare me also."

As soon as she said that, Trina got a hold of herself and redirected all her attention toward the shaman. Trina's father also found a place on the floor right next to me and sat there quietly.

"Please do go on. How can we stop all this from happening? Please tell us," Trina asked.

"I will tell you about a spiritual cleansing that you need to do religiously once you get back home. I will give you small pieces of paper that you need to put under your furniture and authentic sage that you can take back home to burn every single day."

"Alright, and what else? You know that Trina is constantly feeling sick, and her mood shifts so fast. What about that?" Papa asked.

"For that, I have many herbs that I will crush, and you need to have them every single day after dinner. You will see a huge difference in not just your physical health but also your mental health. Just make sure to have it EVERY. SINGLE. DAY," the lady said sternly. "There are also many strange idolized scriptures lying around in your house, as I can see. So be sure to go home and deep clean to find each and every scripture. Without the scriptures out of sight, I cannot begin my spiritual cleansing."

Trina started tearing up again. "What about my son? What if what you are saying is true. How will he get cured of leukemia? I am most worried for him. Please do anything. I beg of you to help stop this atrocity from happening," Trina cried.

"Yes. Yes, wait. For him, it is a tricky case. Since the dark omen is directly toward you, Trina, the weakest links in your family, for example, your lost child and Brandon, are the ones that are the most affected."

"Lord have mercy," Trina's father whispered.

"For him, I will have to read many spells to take off the magic. I cannot assure you anything, which is why I am not saying too much right now. But be patient, and hopefully, the magic will run off."

"Okay, Ma, but who did this? Who is the evil bastard that cast all this magic on my beautiful children?" Papa asked.

"Hmm... I charge extra to reveal the people's identity. And I can surely tell you who did this to you," the lady was adamant about revealing the person's identity.

"Yes, we will pay up, not to worry," I said.

The lady told Trina and me to extend our palms out to her once more, and she took out a large grainy stone from her satchel. She began praying and nodding her head back and forth. If you ask me, it was a little creepy. Her worship lasted a good three minutes, and then she opened her eyes and told us to place our palms on this stone. Trina and I held our hands as tightly as we could and placed the palms of our other hands on the stone. The stone was excruciatingly hot, which was strange because it was not hot, nor did the lady heat it up.

"You see the burning sensation that you are feeling? That is all the magic that these people have done on you. The colder the stone is, the more it shows that there is no black magic or bad omen. Though this stone is clearly telling me that there is a load of magic done on you both," the lady said.

"Who did it?"

"They reside in Northern California." And then the lady shut her eyes again. She held our hands and the rock even tighter. "One couple and one lady, also Vietnamese."

The moment those words left the lady's lips, I knew who it was. As a matter of fact, I was angry. Angry at myself for being this stupid. After all, Trina and I were so suspicious of the fact that it could have been Fran and Victor at first, though we completely forgave them. And it was my bright idea to forgive them and invite them back into our lives. Not Trina's.

"Oh my God, Alex. I can't. It's our friends who are constantly casting all these mad spells on us and constantly have us under their radar. I can't believe it. As a matter of fact, I can. It doesn't come as a surprise to me since Fran became so weird with me from the day we won the lottery," Trina said while she cried even more.

"I know, baby, and I am so sorry for letting you down and inviting them into our lives. Especially after my heart attack, I don't know what I was thinking." As I reflect on this discovery, I can't help but recall the seething rage that consumed me. I was breathing so heavily, though it was a form of anger that had erupted from within, leaving absolutely no reason to feel sorry or restraint. This was just cruel. The sheer injustice that we have endured as a family fueled the flames of my anger, to every fiber of my being burned with hurt and agony. I mean, how could they even think to hurt my family that much? After all that we had done for them? All the good times we had spent with them? I was so hurt I could not.

"Who are these people, Trina?" Papa asked.

"Papa, you know my best friend I always talk about? Fran? Her. And it's so stupid of us because she had given us plenty of reason to cut ties with her."

"Oh no. I always sent blessings to that girl. I thought she was such a poor, sweet soul. I cannot believe this. Cut ties with her immediately," Trina's Father was so shocked; you could just tell by his face. His frown lines almost came down to his nose. I felt bad for him, too, because I knew that he must be feeling so helpless in such a situation.

"After all that we have been through, they felt the need to take away the only thing that brings me happiness. And that is my children... I mean, they didn't even leave my UNBORN child for me," Trina cried. Her screams were so loud that it sent shivers down my spine. I couldn't help but share the same sentiments. I held her on so tightly that I gave her the tightest hug, assuring her that she was not alone. Papa came from the back and held onto us so tightly and began sobbing as well. I really needed Papa's warmth, and I knew that we had him for us for the rest of our lives.

"Okay, quit it, you all. I will constantly pray for you all and hope that all the sorrows go away. Don't lose hope, and keep preaching to your lord. He is the most powerful and forgiving. Count on your blessings, and go on. Though, I must warn you all that the heavy magic that has been cast on you all won't be easy to fight. In many cases, it takes months or even years to cast off. It depends on how frequently the person who is doing it does it. So, be sure to be smart about how you want this to play out. And don't expect such things to become fine for a while right now."

I think that was our cue to leave. By just paying this lady one visit, we just gave our souls the clarity we needed. Though I was extremely angry at that moment, there was nothing I could do till we got back home. We all were so overwhelmed with the information that we got that we were too stunned to speak.

"Thank you so much for giving us so much information. We would have been lost without you," Trina said with so much sincerity. She proceeded to give the old lady a tight hug.

"Yes, thank you so much, Ma. When I saw these two and the state that they were in, I knew that I had to bring them to you as soon as they landed. Forever indebted to your help and generosity. Please take care," Father said as he took his wallet out to pay. He gave her a very generous tip as a thanks for giving us so much information.

"No worries, I pray to God that he brings you both the ease you very much crave. And no more fighting between you two. If there is one thing that you both need to understand, it is that you both need to unite and fight this together. Please take care of Brandon. I will do multiple spiritual cleansings on him, and God willing, he will be alright."

The old lady struggled to get back up on her two feet, so I instantly reached out to help her. Her cold, bony hands clenched onto my arms reminded me of Aunt Mary so much. As soon as she got up, she patted my back and said, "Take care, *con trai, cua toi.*" Which meant that she called me her son. When I turned around to give her a hug as a token of thanks, I saw her small face looking up at me with so much glimmer and hope. Her button eyes were gleaming, giving me so much assurance, the assurance that maybe everything would be okay. After hearing about the turmoil of events, she gave me hope about our tragic situation.

The car ride back home was quiet, to say the least. It was a two-hour drive back home, and we hardly said anything to each other. Trina was sitting in the front seat, next to her dad, and looked out the window the entire time. I could tell that she was utterly distraught after hearing about Brandon. I just knew that there was so much that she needed to take in, how unfortunate she was, and how much she probably hated herself at that exact moment. There was nothing that I could say to her that would bring her the peace and ease that she needed at this moment. I knew that Papa was hurting, too, watching his most cherished person in the world quietly suffering in silence and crying while looking out the window. He couldn't even drive the car properly.

We got back to the house, and as soon as we reached the front lawn, the babysitter came out with Brandon on one side of her hip. My baby, my little one, my world, was so happy to see his parents and grandpa. His face lit up, and he eagerly raised his arms out of pure joy and excitement to see his grandpa and parents.

"Oh my God. Lord, please forgive us," Trina wept. "Alex, how could we have not known that Brandon is sick?"

"Trina, the poor boy is only almost three years of age; I don't see any symptoms of him being ill or anything," I said.

"No…" she cried more. Tears rolled down her cheeks, "Yeah, but how could we have been so careless? I mean, we haven't taken him in for a checkup for a long time. I have been such a bad mother! With all that was happening, I completely forgot about my baby boy. UGH!"

I grabbed Trina by the waist and said, "Hey! Hey, look at me, look up. YOU are nothing but the BEST mother Brandon could ever ask for. You are the best person I have ever known. I can only be half as what you are right now. I know that all this is a little overwhelming, but we will go through it *together*. You understand? Nothing has happened to Brandon, and God forbid anything will ever happen to him. And for God's sake, I don't think the boy has leukemia!!" I made sure to assure Trina that I was there for her at any cost.

Trina sobbed even more, "No, I know, we will fight this together. But everything else the lady said was surely true. I mean, Alex… they didn't even leave my unborn child alone. For fucks SAKE! I want every nerve in my body to not believe what the lady said is true, but I can't help but think otherwise. I'm going to take him for a checkup as soon as we reach home. And I am so so sorry for everything I have put you through. I know I was extremely harsh on you as well. I know I blamed you for the miscarriage I had, and I can't even imagine the agony and scrutiny I put you through. And for that, I am extremely sorry, Alex. You have been nothing but a great sport all this time. Therefore, I apologize; I'm not sure why it took me so long to realize."

"No, it's alright, baby; I know you were hurting. And I knew that I just had to give you space and time. It was a huge bump in our relationship, though we have made it this far," I smiled.

"No, I know that for a fact. Also, what are we going to do about Victor, Michelle, and Fran? We can't let them get away with all of this so easily? I believe that we should confront them," Trina insisted.

"I mean, we'll see when we get back home. I'm not letting them go, either. They messed with our entire family, I mean. Trina, how can someone be this heartless? This heartless to go OUT of their way to ruin someone's family like this? How can they even begin casting this bad omen on us? We have been nothing but good to them? The way we let Fran into our lives, helping her out with everything? And VICTOR? I started to believe that he had finally changed after meeting Michelle. I'm just so angry that I can't find the right words to express my anger, let alone talk about the amount of hurt they have caused me," I said.

"I know, baby, and I knew how attached you got to Victor. And yes, we will figure it out as soon as we get back home."

Trina scooped Brandon from the babysitter and hugged and kissed him as if she was seeing him after years. She held onto him so tightly, with tender hugs and kisses. Trina immersed herself in the tangible presence of Brandon, almost as if the entire world around her had stopped. She squeezed him so tightly to the point where Brandon's cheeks turned red. At that moment, it was quite evident that Trina was not just seeing him, but she was rediscovering the nuances of his perfect being. She checked for any subtle changes in his appearance, the familiarity of his innocent and clean scent, and the rhythm of his laughter. She held onto him for a long time, almost as if she never wanted to let go.

"My baby, my cupcake, my sunshine, what would I do if anything were to happen to you? Alex, come here and look at baby Brandon. Doesn't he feel lighter to you?"

"Trina, my child, now you are just overthinking. Stop it, and all will be well. Ma said it herself!" Father said.

"Yes, Trina, that's a bit much. Now, we'll take him to the best doctor when we go back home. Don't you worry, okay?" I added.

We all sat in Father's living room, and he prepared us some tea and snacks. After all the exhaustion, this was exactly what I needed.

"Alex, tell me. Who are Victor and Michel? I am confused," Papa asked.

"Huh, where do I start? So basically, after we won the lottery, Trina's friend Fran came over one day, and she introduced us to Victor. At first, I thought he was a very handsome, cool guy who had a sick mansion on the outskirts with a lavish vineyard. He was very nice and keen on becoming friends at first, so that's how we became friends. After a very long time, I became super friendly with someone, and that was Victor. Then, a few months later, came Michelle, Victor's girlfriend, who was also super sweet at first. We all became super close, including Trina, because, as you know, there were very few acquaintances that you could relate to in such a small town," I said.

"Oh, I see, see, that was what was wrong. They knew you won the lottery, and they had eyes on the prize from day one. Hmm…" Papa said.

"Yeah! That's exactly it. And funny enough, after finding out that Aunt Mary had also left me a fraction of her wealth, they became even more greedy and strange."

"Yeah, Dad. When we were staying at Victor's, before eating dinner, Michelle made us read some strange scripture out loud. And all this time, I thought that it was some family tradition that she followed, but I guess not. Surprisingly, Michelle and Victor DID NOT chant the same stuff Alex and I chanted. It was so so strange. I'm not sure how I didn't catch onto that."

"Oh my. What did the scripture say? That is pure evil!" Father questioned.

"It said some strange gibberish in Latin, I believe," I said.

As he picked up his teacup, he paused. "In Latin? That is crazy because the strongest magic in my knowledge is actually done in Latin. Promise me one thing, you both. Now that you have moved to Florida, please cut all ties with these people. No matter how sorry you feel for them. Promise me," Papa uttered anxiously.

"Yes, of course, Dad, they are out of our lives completely," Trina said.

"Yeah, and be sure to get your house deeply cleaned, as Ma was saying. You never know what you will find. Strange scriptures or idols."

Trina laid back on the cozy couch, and I could just tell that her mom's protective radar was constantly on. She was thinking of the best alternatives to tackle the situation. It was just annoying that this situation was out of her hands completely. There wasn't anything that she could have done to fix the situation for the better.

"Alex, I am so worried. Something will happen to Brandon, my gut is telling me. I mean, how can we protect our baby? How can you not be freaking out right now? I don't know how I will be able to sleep at night, knowing that my son is in jeopardy," Trina gripped my hand with intense firmness. She hadn't done that in so long.

"Baby, I love you. You just need to understand that nothing will happen to Brandon. We are constantly watching him and with him. I will assure you that nothing will happen to our beautiful baby boy."

"Yeah, I hope so. The only thing that is stressing me out is that whatever magic they cast on me before nearly broke me. I got so sick, and I lost my second unborn baby. Therefore, whatever they are doing is very strong," Trina nervously said.

"Trina, you know when I went outside for a bit? When you guys were sitting with the old lady? You don't know what happened," I said.

"What. What happened, Alex?" Trina asked.

"I didn't want to tell you this, although when I went outside, it was because I couldn't breathe. There was a lot of pain in my chest and my left arm, and I thought I was having another stroke. I ran outside to the car to get some fresh air. And when my breathing declined, I looked for aspirin in your bag, and thank God I found it. I don't know what I would've done otherwise," I said to Trina.

"Lord. Alex. Why didn't you tell me? Do you know how dangerous that is? Especially because you already had a heart attack before. I can't believe you didn't tell me. Come, let's go to the ER right now," Trina insisted.

"No, Trina. With so much that is going on, I don't think I should make this about me. And I took the aspirin; I don't think it should be a problem."

It was one of the longest days I have had in a while; it felt as if this day couldn't get any worse. I felt as if everything in the universe began to hate me. Every little discrepancy, to nuisance, was making my patience levels run extremely thin. All I wanted to do at the time was run outside and shout from the top of my lungs. An overpowering surge of emotions came rushing, and I yearned to shout so loudly that everyone in this universe, as well as the heavens, could hear me out so that God himself could ask me what was wrong. It wasn't just about being loud and making a sound; it was just a proclamation that someone could hear me and feel what I was going through.

I mean, was that what winning the lottery gets to you? For you to become so miserable that you find it hard to even live one day in peace? For the closest loved ones to use you and have bad intentions toward you? I mean, yeah, people get jealous, though will they also go to such extreme lengths to cast black magic spells on you??? I mean, it's no wonder why so many rich people are so unhappy. Money doesn't solve anything. I mean, the problems that I had, it surely couldn't. I was a complete mess. I was feeling like shit.

Chapter Eleven — Trina, My Dear Wife

After spending a much-needed break in Vietnam for about two weeks, Trina and I decided to head back to Florida. I would have preferred to stay in Vietnam for a longer period, although Trina's work had to call us back. Besides, Ma, the old lady, told us that her spiritual cleansing process would only start once we traveled back to our home in Florida. So, we had to go back in order for things to get back to normal. The only thing that constantly kept bothering me was Brandon's health. We decided that we would have him consulted by one of the best doctors in Florida. Though we were packing up our things at the time, it was one of the most sentimental and emotional times I have witnessed to date.

I recall Trina's father being so nervous about sending us back. He kept saying, "Please stay for a bit," and "My home is always open to you both here, don't leave." He was so adamant about us staying and waiting the entire process out. He was worried that the spiritual cleansing and one visit to Ma weren't enough. Papa wanted us to go back to her for another visit because he was even more stressed than us about this entire situation. I could just tell by his frown lines creasing all the way down to his brow bone. As much as I loved and appreciated Papa's love and affection toward us, I think it was high time that we headed back to Florida to face the real world.

As much as I wanted Trina and me to stop fighting and arguing for God's know-what reason. Unfortunately, that didn't end. She still had mad trust issues with me and blamed me for the randomest reasons possible. She suddenly became extremely over-protective of Brandon, and she suddenly had a problem with me, even holding him. I mean, I am his father, and I have all the rights in the world to hold my child and take him out. I didn't expect nor appreciate this behavior from Trina at all. Nor did papa. It was as if, at any given moment when I felt like holding my child, she would automatically assume that Brandon would break. However, I don't blame her either since everything was very recent, and she's extremely nervous about Brandon getting leukemia.

We packed our bags, and Papa insisted that he drop us off at the airport. My heart was so heavy; one part of me was excited to head back and confront Victor, Michelle, and Fran, but the other part of me was nervous about what the future holds for us. I prayed to God so much that please don't let it not be more bad news. We had so much on our plate, and this entire dark omen and black magic was definitely stressing me out. I mean, what if Ma was unable to reverse the magic? What is supposed to happen then?

On our way to the airport, it was a bittersweet feeling. I didn't want to leave, but it's not like we could stay in Vietnam forever. All I know is that the magic can't be done from overseas because, as far as I know, magic can't be traveled as long as There's a body of water in the middle. Though, as we reside in Florida now, I am not so sure. There isn't a body of water in the middle; therefore, even if they decide to do magic on us, it will most likely conform. I could tell that Papa was also super nervous about sending us back to the United States because he kept saying:

"Trina, my baby, I don't want you to lose hope.

Please have faith in Ma, and trust me, your family is in no jeopardy. I can vouch for that," Papa said as he hastened onto the steering wheel.

"I hope so, Dad. Though, please take care of yourself here. And don't forget your diabetic medicine. I don't want you to forget about your health, in the matters of ours. We will be fine. Promise me?" Trina said in a stern tone.

"Yes, I promise, my child. Although, promise me that you won't fight with Alex?" Papa asked.

"Wha…? Ugh!! Why are you only telling me this? Do you think I'm the one always stirring the pot? Well, you need to understand that Alex is also no saint," Trina said.

Papa and I both chuckled for a good two minutes straight.

"Well said, Papa!! I second you on that," I chimed in.

"Alex? Stop it," Trina said.

"What? I'm not saying anything. It's Papa. He's the third party here, and he sees all," I said in a sweet voice.

"WELL, no need to bring him into this. He doesn't know everything. It's whatever; we can handle it when we're back in Florida," Trina said.

"Handle what? There's more? For God's sake,"

I sighed.

"Trina… let the poor man breathe. We all have had a heck of a couple of days. This is no time to fight over useless things," Papa said as he bellowed in a voice that echoed through the car.

"Yeah, Trina," I was also tired of the persistent fighting that we have been doing in Florida, and I have had enough. And I knew that the second we go back, the same drama is most likely to start again. I thought we were over all the constant fighting and that we needed to be there for Brandon.

We reached the airport, and the moment we arrived, it was extremely gloomy. Papa said it was most likely to rain, though I was hoping that it wouldn't because it was time to head back to the United States. It was almost as if the weather was also sad for us to leave. Was it a sign? I'm not sure. Brandon was sleeping in the back seat, clenched onto Trina, completely lost as to what was happening. I gave Papa the tightest hug as a token of gratitude for all that he has done for us this entire time. If it weren't for him, Trina and I would be utterly lost in life. He has been our pillar of strength, and after Aunt Mary's demise, he's the only real family I have. He's not just my father-in-law, but he's a long-lost best friend that I have longed to have for the longest time. Papa let us stay in his beautiful home for three weeks without any questions asked. I took out all the luggage from the trunk while Brandon was in Trina's arms.

"Thank you, Papa. Without you, Trina and I would be so lost. I can't thank you enough, and I don't even have the right words to tell you how much you mean to me." I was about to tear up, and I don't know what got into me, though I was so emotional the entire time.

"Oh no, Alex! Don't do this to me. Don't make it even harder than it is to say bye to you guys. I have only you guys. Please take extra care of Brandon and give him my love every night."

"Papa, promise me that you will come and visit us soon. You know you can come *whenever* you want. I will also book you a flight ticket," I insisted.

"Oh no, Alex, that's quite alright. But I will definitely come in the following months. I want to check up on you a lot, especially Brandon. I want to see how he will be doing," Papa said.

"Papa, I love you so much. And I thank God every single day for blessing me with a father like you. Please never forget that. And yes, I second Alex. Why can't you come and stay with us soon?" Trina retorted toward her father, her eyes sparkling with a mix of emotions, of defiance and affection. "Oh, Papa, I'm going to miss you so very much." Despite Trina expressing her love toward her father, a sudden surge of warmth and sadness overcame her, prompting her to grasp onto her father a little tighter.

The embrace spoke volumes.

Papa sniffled, "Now, go on, you two. Otherwise, you will miss your flight. I will come and meet you both soon." He proceeded to give baby Brandon a kiss and patted his head as a blessing.

I towed the luggage trolley and headed toward the check-in gate, and as I was transcending toward the check-in gate, the weight of the heavy suitcases seemed to mirror the heaviness that was settling in my chest. As we continued on the path to check in, the distance between Papa and us widened. He began to look smaller and smaller against the backdrop of the bustling crowd behind him. Each step toward the check-in gate felt like a step away from the familiar, and the absolute gravity of the moment sank in as I turned back for a brief glance. I now realized that it was Trina, Brandon, and I against the world.

We checked in, and we had an hour to kill before our flight boarded. Trina had just called to tell Papa that everything was alright. Brandon had woken up now, and he was playing around the coffee house where we decided to spend an hour before the flight.

"Alex, Michelle keeps asking me when we're heading back. She has called me three times now. What should I do?" Trina asked as she held up her phone to show me.

"Oh my God. What's wrong with her? Please get rid of her immediately. We don't want anything to do with her anymore," I said.

"No, I know, but how can I just automatically block her? And also, don't you want to confront them? I think we should give in so that they assume that everything is normal for now," Trina said.

"Yeah, you're actually right. Just tell her that we will be back in a week. Make sure you don't give her any other details," I said.

"Gotcha," Trina got up with a coffee in her other hand, and she called Michelle back. I kept my eye on Brandon, making sure that he was alright.

The time flew by, and we were on the plane headed toward Florida. As I sat there on the window aisle, I looked out the window and let out a serious prayer. I held my hands together, and I asked God to please keep my little family in his protection. I know I haven't been the best Christian, and please forgive me if I had any bad intentions toward anyone. I told him to look after baby Brandon the most because the moment we get back to Florida, he will be going for a checkup. I wanted Ma to be wrong so badly, and there is no way she can be right about this.

After about 18 hours, we finally reached Florida, and honestly, it felt good to be back under the sun and in tropical weather. As soon as we got out of the airport, a sudden wave of heat hit us, welcoming us to the bipolar yet warm city that we love. Not gonna lie. It felt good to be back. We took an Uber back home, and it had been almost a month since we got back home. Our doorman, Mark, was so happy to see us.

"Sir! You are finally back. I am so glad. I am happy to assist. How was Vietnam?"

"Mark! What can I say? It was a wonderful treat. We spent time at Trina's family home and had a great time with her father. How are you?" I asked.

"I've been better. Haha. Missed Brandon out here a lot; without him, there was utter silence in the entire building," he said.

"Glad to hear it! Well, he's back now, and he's all yours!" I said delightfully. Mark went on to pick Brandon up and give him a hug.

"Please put him down," Trina said as she sneered an eye roll and said dismissively.

"Oh," Mark quietly put Brandon down and was extremely confused as to what had just happened. He didn't say anything and walked past Trina and me.

"Trina, that was extremely rude; I don't expect you to be rude to Mark," I said.

"What? How was that rude? I just asked him not to pick him up. I don't want Brandon to get injured or bruised. Ma said that he has leukemia, for crying out loud! It's not a joke!"

"Alright, but it's not like he's going to break or something simply because somebody picks him up. You do, too. So let it go," I said in a stern tone.

"Alex. I am very fatigued and exhausted. *Don't* get me started again, okay? I don't have it in me to argue. So shut your trap," Trina said.

"Excuse me? I am tired as well; there is no need to be rude to me either. I have had it with you and your rude behavior toward me," I said.

"What behavior are you talking about? You're the one who ratted me out in front of my own Papa.

What about that? I didn't say a thing to him!!" she jumped.

"Yes, Trina, because I had to. You said some really rude things, and just because I love you so much doesn't mean I'm going to take your shit all the time," I screamed. "Plus, I thought we were over?" I added.

"We aren't over shit. It's just super pissing off, the fact that you never seem to understand anything that I'm going through or how I'm feeling or anything," Trina cried. "It's like you're just there in the background; you're never there for me emotionally."

As soon as Trina said this, I felt very horrible. An overwhelming sense of hurt and self-doubt washed over me, causing me a sense of unease. At that moment, I almost instantly began to question the foundation of our entire relationship. The only question that kept ringing inside my head was, "Have I always been like this? Has she always thought of me being this useless?" I mean, in a way, she was calling me a complete floozy. All I have ever thought of doing is for her and our family. Why is she questioning my integrity? The disparity between my intentions and her perception sowed utter confusion and self- reflection, almost prompting me to reevaluate the very essence of who I thought in my wife's eyes.

"Trina, you're being very rude to me. And I don't appreciate this at all," I said.

"I don't care!! I'm just telling you how I feel. And if you can't take that, then I don't know what to say to you," she said.

"But I don't know where to go from here. Like we just got back home, and from all the information we have learned about in Vietnam, I thought we would come together, and we're going to figure it out together also?"

"Okay, but that doesn't rule out the fact that you have been so lost and bewildered about my feelings and my sentiments," Trina said.

"Trina, but I don't know which sentiments you're talking about because, as far as I know, I have been here for you through hours' end. I don't have friends, I don't go out, I don't have a social life, so I don't know what you're going on about," I expressed my concern because she was questioning my entire character at this point.

"Yeah, I know, but I'm not sure what I'm feeling these days. It's weird. Please just give me some space, and I'll be fine in a few days."

We reached Florida on Tuesday morning, and it was Thursday morning when Trina and I had another conversation after that one when we came back. After that conversation that we had, we hadn't spoken, and as she requested that I stay out of her hair, I frankly did.

"Alex, I booked a consultation appointment with Dr. Frank Carnegie, which took me weeks to score, so I'm taking Brandon there today. So, do you want to come with us?" Trina asked. She was surprisingly nice.

"Let me look at my schedule for today, and let me get back to you."

Trina scoffed, "What? You can't sacrifice your book club for your son's appointment? How sad…"

"Trina, excuse you. All I needed to check was whether I didn't have a meeting with the landlord about the houses we had given up on rent. Nothing else. Geez," I said.

"Yeah, right."

"I don't know why you're so quick to pounce. I didn't say anything," I said, and she rolled her eyes again.

I drove us to the doctor, which was about 30 minutes away from our apartment building, and the entire car ride was very quiet. I could only hear Brandon's cooing and his amazement toward the greenery outside. Driving to the hospital was very nerve-wracking because this was the day we were going to find out about Brandon. I was confident that the doctors would only have positive things to say about our baby boy. Although Trina had a motherly instinct that what Ma said would be spot on and true,

As soon as we met Dr. Frank, he was very delightful. He assured us that anything we wanted to ask him, we could. He also said that by the looks of Brandon, physically, he seems perfectly fine.

"His weight seems to be perfectly fine. Perfect for a 3-and-a-half-year-old; as for his blood sample, I will take that right now so that we can analyze his blood work. Please try to retort his attention toward you guys so he doesn't panic when he sees the needle," Dr. Frank asked politely.

He took out Brandon's blood so carefully that Brandon didn't even notice. Trina kept him busy by going for ice cream later on, which made him extremely excited.

"Alright, that was a breeze. You've got a very patient kid! Okay. So, the blood samples will come back from the lab in about a week, so we will know if your son has been diagnosed with leukemia or not. Fingers crossed," Dr. Frank said.

"Thank you so much, Doc. Is there anything that we should take care of? Or be cautious about?" Trina asked.

"Um, not really. Just be sure to look out for symptoms," Dr. Frank said.

"Symptoms like what? Might I ask?" I said.

"Tiredness, or unannounced weakness. Or even mouth sores or fevers that jump up unannounced."

"Alright, thank you, Doc. Is there any way that the test results can come a little faster?" Trina asked.

"No, I'm afraid not. The lab testing happens in outer state labs, which takes time to come back to the city. I will have my PA call you as soon as they get back," he said.

We headed back home, and it was time for Trina to head back to her job after the month-long vacation that she had taken. I was sitting on the couch adjacent to the kitchen island, and I had just put on the news. I had whipped up my forever favorite Trader Joe's dumplings and prepared myself a green tea, and Brandon was playing on the iPad. As soon as Trina entered the kitchen to fill up her water bottle, I heard a clucking voice, which I ignored.

"Hey baby, when will you be back? I can prepare dinner for us," I said as I stared at the TV screen. After a minute of no response, I turned around and saw Trina lying on the floor, completely passed out.

A rush of immediate concern surged through me, seeing Trina unconscious on the floor. I scurried toward her, and my heart was pounding outside my chest. I kneeled right beside her, took her water bottle, and sprayed some water onto her. I gently began to call her name, trying to rouse her almost immediately. Brandon slowly walked toward us, also as confused as I was as to what was going on, and started calling for his mother. The seconds that felt like an eternity almost ended, and Trina slowly regained her consciousness; a mixture of relief and panic washed all over me.

Chapter Twelve — The Road Back to Normality

Trina's well-being was at the top of my concerns at that moment. I thought that a visit that we paid to Ma would help matters get better, although they clearly hadn't. And it was so sad to see that Trina was the one mainly getting affected by this evil magic the most. As soon as she woke up, I picked her up and took her to our room so she could have some rest. I grabbed cold, icy water from our fridge and reached for the medicines that were kept on the bathroom shelf. I made sure that she had everything she needed because passing out like this in broad daylight was not safe. I decided to call Papa as soon as Trina felt a little better.

"Hey, Papa! How are you?"

"Hello, Alex. I'm alive and well! Praise the lord. How are you all holding up? How does it feel to get back home? Are you guys in a better state?" Papa asked in a worried manner.

"Uh… Yeah, sort of," I said. I was a little hesitant to tell him about Trina because I knew that he would freak out after all the recent incidents.

"No, Alex. You seem a little confused; tell me what has happened? I can tell by your voice," Papa urged.

"Uhh, basically, Trina and I thought that since we were back from Vietnam and had paid a visit to Ma, things would get better. Although…" Papa cut me off.

"WHAT HAPPENED? IS IT BRANDON?" he shouted.

"No, no, no, Papa!! Relax, Brandon's reports haven't come back yet. Although, I am really worried for Trina. She was heading to work just now, and as she was packing her things up, she just fell. Point blank. And it's not even like she was feeling sick or anything. She was perfectly fine, and yet this happened to her. So could you please contact Ma and ask her what is happening? I thought all the magic would be reversed? I am so confused, and I am genuinely so sick of all these traumatic things happening to us as a family," I said.

"Oh my… Still? Dear Lord! Okay, I will call Ma up immediately and ask her. Also, Alex, have you been burning the sage, and has Trina been eating the medicine Ma had given her to eat every single day?"

"Oh shit, Papa, I don't think that she has been having the medicine at all. It must have completely slipped her mind. Though, now, I will make sure that she does," I said.

"Alex??? What are you guys waiting for? This is not something to slack about! And when are we hearing back from Brandon's doctor? I must know, I am praying for my grandchild continuously," Papa said.

"Um, we hear back from Brandon's doctor in two days. Please pray, Papa, and pray and hope for the best for our son," I said.

"Of course, I am continuously praying for your and your family's well-being, Alex. Don't you ever forget that?"

After having this conversation with Papa, I immediately started looking for Trina's medicine that Ma had given her. I asked her where she kept it, and since she was hazed, Trina wasn't much help. I searched our entire apartment and finally found them in Trina's purse, which gave me an instant relief. I think she was planning on taking them after heading to work. I took two of the pills outside, and they had a distinct smell. I grabbed a bottle of water from the fridge and headed toward our room. I told Trina to get up and have these pills instantly and immediately looked at the time. It was exactly 10:30 am, and I made sure to tell her to have the medicine at the same time the next day.

After that, Trina decided to take a nap for a bit while I watched Brandon watching "*Despicable Me*." It was so cute. All his attention was directed toward the yellow minions moving, and it was so wholesome. In a way, I was glad that Brandon was still a young toddler during this period of our lives because there is so much that is happening. I would never want my child to witness any of the evil things that were happening to us. If he were a little older, he would definitely start questioning all the strange behavior and activities that were happening in our house.

Brandon would witness all the fights Trina and I had, which would take such a horrible toll on his mental health. Especially, Aunt Mary's passing and our big move to Florida would have really tortured him.

Two days passed at the speed of light, and it was finally time for us to put up Brandon's tests. Today was the day that Trina and I were anxiously waiting for because we would finally find out about Brandon's well-being. I'm not sure how we passed the time in these two weeks, although it was definitely a whirlwind of emotions. Trina drove us to the hospital, and the doctor called us in at 11:30. We made sure to leave for the hospital on time since Brandon's doctor was very busy, and he refused to wait for any of his patients.

On our way to the hospital, I had this uneasy feeling of sadness and somberness that took over my entire mood. I kept thinking to myself, like, what has our destiny gotten to us? Nothing in this world matters to me other than finding out whether or not my child is okay. So why do we spend so much time worrying about things in this life? Why do we worry about money or what others think of us so much? It's not right. I had this uneasy feeling that I was about to find out something very terrible. My heart was palpitating fast, and I know Trina's was too. I just didn't want to say anything because I knew that she would lash out at me like this.

We met with Brandon's doctor, Dr. Frank, and he was being wonderful. He asked how Trina and I were doing and took us to his premises. Brandon was leaning onto my shoulder, with his back toward Dr. Frank.

"Could you just please put Brandon down? I need to see how he is doing," Dr. Frank said.

"Of course," I said. I placed Brandon on the hospital bed, which he was getting annoyed at. He lifted up his arms and began to cry because he wanted me to hold him up again.

Dr. Frank searched for Brandon's file, which only took about a second.

"You know this reached this morning only, and I am glad that you guys have come this fast," Dr. Frank said.

My heart fell to my stomach because this is one thing you hear once there is something followed by bad news. Trina took a deep breath and said, "Let's hear it, Doctor."

"Well, I went over Brandon's reports, and I am so sorry to say that he has been diagnosed with Leukemia. As you can see in this report, he has an abnormal amount of white blood cells and significantly low red blood cells. A normal functioning child at Brandon's age must have about 5.5 million red blood cells and a healthy amount of white cells to fight this disease. Unfortunately, he doesn't have that. At Brandon's age, it is also very easy for him to contract bone marrow because this is his growing age, where his bones and physical self are growing. I am so very sorry," Dr. Frank said.

As soon as he said this, it was like another hard punch in the gut. I was so extremely disappointed, though I was not surprised. It was as if this entire universe was against us three, where it just wanted to eat us up.

Trina started to stutter, fighting all her will not to start crying again. "Well, I'm sure this has to be a mistake, Dr. Frank? I mean, look at Brandon; he's physically perfectly alright. I see no signs of weakness at all? Is there any way to reverse it? I mean, there has to be a chance that this is a complete mistake!!!" Trina was hyperventilating.

"Ms. Trina, I am so sorry. I know this is the last thing any parent would want to hear, although the reports don't lie. I had them tested in the best facility there is. Although there are so many treatments that your son will undergo to cure his illness. Brandon may not show physical signs or symptoms, although they will definitely catch onto him soon enough," Dr. Frank said politely.

"What other alternatives do we have? And can you please guide us with what procedure we should follow next?" I said while holding all my emotions.

"Well, the next order of business would be to undergo a bone marrow aspiration or biopsy to confirm whether the blood cells have reached his bones, which causes the cancer. And as you guys are stating, Brandon has shown no sort of symptoms up till now, and I don't believe that it has," Dr. Frank said.

"My child will have to go through a biopsy?

That is absurd," Trina shouted.

I walked aside to the hospital bed to be there for her during this time. I held her, and she started bawling. Trina was not okay. I gave her the tightest hug I could possibly give and kept whispering in her ear, "Trina, we will get through this. You and I will fight for our baby boy. There must be some way he would get cured. Don't you freak out just yet? There is a lot of fight left." Trina was panting so much that it was almost as if I could hear her heart thumping outside her chest. Her brittle little body was shaking so much.

"I will give you two a moment. Just know that you have come to the right place and that this hospital is the best place to get treatment. Though it will be a sturdy process. You both, as parents, have to be here for your baby boy and trust the process. With time, Brandon will be fine," Dr. Frank said.

There was nothing else we could do at that moment. Dr. Frank prescribed Brandon some medicine to take and specifically asked us to keep updating him on Brandon's health. Trina went to the counter to schedule the biopsy that would be led by Dr. Frank himself.

On our way back from the hospital, I recall Trina and I being furious. Not at everything that was happening around us, mainly on all that Victor, Fran, and Michelle had brought upon us. I mean, all this is beyond anyone's control, and how are we ever going to recover from it? It was understandable if they implemented all this magic on Trina and me, but Brandon? I was enraging with anger, and I wanted to punch Victor's head open. If I hadn't invited him over to my house after my heart attack, then I believe that none of this would ever happen. I truly believe that all of this happened because of me, and I am the only one to blame. I decided to have a conversation with Trina to let all my feelings out and tell her how I have been feeling throughout all of this.

"Hey Trina, I just want to get something off my chest, and I have been thinking like this for the longest period," I said.

"I'm not in the mood, Alex," Trina said.

"No, I just want to get something off my chest for the longest time now, and now I believe that you should be hearing it from me," I said.

"Okay, go on," Trina said.

"I think I made the biggest mistake of my life by inviting these people back into our lives after my heart attack. If I hadn't done this, none of this would be happening, and we all would be in such a better place than this. I just want you to know that you shouldn't be worrying about how you haven't been a good person or a bad mom in this life because you genuinely have. I believe that all of this is my doing, and I will now take matters into my own hands," I signed.

"No, Alex, I don't agree. You need to stop blaming yourself for all that has happened. It's not because of you; if anything, I believe that the lottery is what brought an awful sort of bad luck. So don't be hard on yourself and think that all this happened because of you because it didn't," Trina said.

"Yeah, but now everything is clear to me. I know what needs to be done now," I said.

"What needs to be done? What are you planning on doing, Alex?" Trina was worried.

"No, I just want to go back home and confront Victor, Fran, and Michelle. It's only because of them that we are suffering like this. And I believe that they should be held accountable," I said.

"No, Alex, those people are dangerous. If you confront them, then Victor can easily harm you, and I don't want that," Trina uttered.

"TRINA! Do you just want me to sit on the sidelines and watch what they will do next? No, we have to confront them! We have to make them realize what they have done. To make them realize that they will go to hell for all their doings. We have to make them realize that they will NEED TO PAY FOR THEIR ACTIONS!" I shouted. I was so furious that if I were able to shoot Victor on point blank, I would.

"Hey, hey, hey, hey, listen to me. Calm down. We will take care of this when we get back home. I am not letting you go alone, which is why I will come with you. I am not letting you do this alone. They are so dangerous," Trina said.

Now that I had Trina's approval, I realized that it was time to book our flights to Northern California once again. There was so much business that needed to be taken care of, and I won't get proper peace till I confront those pieces of shit. There was no more remorse left in my body anymore. I knew what had to be done, and I would happily take care of it. I decided to book our tickets back home for the next day since it was a weekend. Trina and I decided to leave Friday morning and catch whoever unannounced around town since it's really small. I knew that I would catch Michelle or Victor at the Bistro or strolling around the park. Trina told Brandon's trusted babysitter to come and watch him for three days since we were out of town. I had no worries leaving Brandon in the hands of Elizabeth because she was so reliable and trusted for generations.

Trina and I caught a flight the next day, and it was safe to say that this was the fastest we have decided to hop on from city to city. We hopped on the plane Friday morning and reached back home around 4 pm. I decided to book an Airbnb, which was a two- minute walking distance from our old home. It was the safest neighborhood in the city, and Trina and I felt the safest there. To be honest, I wasn't exactly sure how to confront these two, although Trina and I decided that we should just show up at their house in order to confront them. We need to catch them off guard and confront them with all that they have done.

The moment we landed back home, none of us were at ease; despite the Airbnb being an exquisite retreat home, Trina and I just had one thing on our minds. We chose to freshen up, unpack our belongings for three days, and decided to head out to the Bistro for a quick snack. Nobody knew that we were in town, and I knew for a fact that somebody interesting would definitely spot us back home.

We still had our car from back home, which Trina and I decided not to sell when we were moving. We headed toward the Bistro, and honestly, it felt good to be there. Honestly, it's always refreshing to be back on these streets once again. We reached the Bistro, and surprisingly, it was packed. There wasn't even one place to sit, and I knew that we would bump into someone. All of a sudden, we were greeted by someone right behind us. And it was Fran.

"Oh my god! Trina, when did you get back? I am so delighted to see you!! When did you get back?" Fran said in her squeaky voice.

"Hi, Fran. Yeah, Alex and I have come back for business." Trina was very cold from the start.

"Oh, no way! What kind of business?" Fran was insinuating.

"Just some random things. Plus, we wanted to come by since we haven't in quite a while," Trina said.

"Oh, sweet! Where are you staying? I can come by to drop a few goodies," Fran said.

"No, that's alright. We're good," Trina said. While I was standing at the back, pretending like I wasn't listening to the awkward conversation they were having.

Trina walked right in front, completely ignoring Fran, which I was so proud of her for doing. We transcended toward the main reception counter of the Bistro and asked for a table. Watching Fran after so long definitely made me reminisce about the old days when she used to do all sorts of evil things. We got a table about ten minutes later and were seated. Trina and I had a very delightful meal, which reminded me of the good old days at the Bistro. I had their best fish and chips, and Trina ordered pasta. It's quite funny because it reminded me of Trina and me when we were in high school. It was all good vibes.

After having a delightful meal at the Bistro, we decided to finally confront Victor and Michelle. I'm not sure whether or not Fran had warned them before, but I will take my chances. I was furious; there was nothing that could stop me at that time.

It was quarter to seven when Trina and I drove up to Victor's mansion, and the only thing running through my head was Brandon. I couldn't possibly do anything to this guy that would reverse my baby boy's illness, although I knew that nothing would give me solace than to get revenge.

113

Chapter Thirteen — The Revenge

It was quarter to 8 when Trina and I wrapped up our meal at the bistro and headed toward Victor and Michelle's house. It was a thirty-minute ride from the bistro since Victor lived a little outside town. I was not exactly sure how to go about the situation since I only wanted to punch Victor's face, especially because of all the red flags he had shown me before. The way Trina and I buckled up in the car was definitely a scene that reminded me of Bonnie and Clyde. I was so appreciative of how Trina was backing me up on this, and it made my feelings feel so valid. She had the same insane, raging anger shielded on her chest, just like I did.

The closer we were getting to Victor's house, the more I was grasping the steering wheel even tighter because there was so much anger and rage within me. All the pain and misery that he had put my family through is something I wouldn't even wish on my biggest enemy. If Victor and Michelle were to get married and have children, I wouldn't wish this upon their children as well. Since I am a human, whatever their parents decide to do are consequences only they should sow. Victor went after my unborn child, Brandon, and my wife. I recall the GPS that was driving us to Victor's house was taking forever; my chest started feeling a little heavy because I was extremely nervous. I was hoping that he didn't have any unwanted guests because this would entirely ruin my chance of getting back at him.

We finally reached his house, and because I was arriving there after a while, it felt surreal. All the great times we had spent together, all the football games, parties, and dinners were all coming back to me. Safe to say that it was a whirlwind of emotions. Regardless of all the rage and anger that was inside me, such situations have the complete potential to get the best of you. It tests your strength and emotions, almost like a heartbreak. You know, everyone talks about relationships and heartbreak, although I believe that what's even harder than heartbreak is when two really close friends end their friendship. However, in this case, it was over forever and cannot be fixed even if Victor and Michelle try a thousand times and over.

Trina got out of the car and headed toward the entrance, and I immediately followed. I had parked the car two cars down in case they peeked through the window to see who it was. As I stood there with Trina, the air around me filled up with tension and anxiety, and my heart raced uncontrollably, almost as if it was trying to escape my chest. Beating so very fast. The presence of Trina seemed to awaken a primal force within me, a force I knew had the utmost potential to become violent and strange. Almost an uneasy knot tightened in the pit of my stomach, and I couldn't shake the feeling that I was teetering. Victor's house was so close to us, and we were patiently waiting outside. I glanced at Trina, and I was so sure that she was nervous, too. I wasn't sure if I wanted to put her through this, although there was nothing I could do. Her eyes held a magnetic pull that drew me in and also brought me extreme solace and composure during this time. I also sensed the impending storm that lurked between the surface.

She stood there with a stern attitude and the strongest posture. Her facial expressions and posture bespoke all her resilience and strength during her toughest times, and that spoke volumes. I was so proud of my baby. The feeling was unexplainable.

Trina rang the doorbell, and now it was just the waiting game.

The creak of the door hinged and echoed through the hallway as Michelle swung it open with a welcoming smile playing on her lips initially. The warmth in her expression, however, quickly gave way to a sudden cold chill, as if an unseen shadow had cast its darkness across her small features. Due to the shock, Michelle's eyes widened for a moment, almost screaming a subtle shift in emotion. The moment she laid eyes on Trina, Trina gave her the fakest smile. In the suspense of that moment, the tension in the room became palpable. The air was suddenly mixed with anticipation and trepidation, as though we all saw a ghost amongst us. The profound shift in Michelle's demeanor added an eerie layer to the suspense.

The moment Michelle laid eyes on Trina, she said, "Oh, Hi! What a lovely surprise. I wasn't expecting you guys today. When did you guys come back?"

With the fakest attitude and energy. Trina walked past her and said, "Yeah, What a wonderful surprise, Michelle."

Almost instantly, I heard Victor asking Michelle, "Honey, who is it?" which instantly got me even more angry than I was. I couldn't stand that man.

We both walked into their home uninvited, which felt almost illegal. Michelle refused to respond to Victor, but by the time I caught up and paved my way through their living room upon crossing the threshold, the warm embrace of the familiar and memories hit me all of a sudden. It was pretty evident that Michelle and Victor were adorned with the festive spirit of throwing a lavish dinner. The dining table, the main centerpiece, was carefully arranged with an assortment of evergreen branches, with glistening silver and gold ornaments spread out around it so carefully. There were six large candles beautifully kept in the middle of the dinner table, already lit since I'm assuming that their guests were about to arrive. The dinnerware gleamed with holiday sophistication, each plate meticulously positioned with precision. Silverware lay in perfect alignment beside crystal clear glasses, ready to clink in the midst of a celebration. The napkins that were set beside them had intricate embroidery of snowflakes, just perfect for the celebration.

We walked into their living room, and there I caught Victor watching TV, all dressed in an all-white linen outfit with a navy blue tweed jacket on top. The moment Victor saw me, I knew his heart flushed. I was the last person on earth that he probably expected to see through the door. As our eyes locked, a moment in time froze. His expression, which was initially composed, betrayed a sudden acceleration of his heartbeat. That instant, I believe that he knew that shit was going to go down. I think that he saw my facial expressions and realized that I was in no mood to chat or sit down and have a conversation. I paved my way toward his couch and asked, "Another dinner party to fuck someone else's lives up now?"

"Alex!! What a surprise!! What makes you come here?" Victor asked calmly.

"No reason, I just wanted to have a conversation, and I hope I am not interrupting." The rage inside me was getting worse and worse.

"Yeah, I am a little busy. You should've called before coming. And what do you mean by ruining someone else's life up now? What is that about?" he insinuated.

The moment I heard those words, a sense of extreme anger rushed all over me. I took my right fist and, with all the anger that was building up inside me, found Victor's face. The moment my fist landed on Victor's face, he fell backward, and I went onto him again. His eyes widened in surprise and pain as he staggered backward, unprepared for the sudden eruption of anger. Without any hesitation, I refused to back down. I pressed on, fueled and angered by the intensity of the emotions surging within me, ready for any reaction that he was going to clap back with.

That instant after I went in with the second punch, my knuckles started to crackle, leaving them extremely red and soar. I believe that I aimed right at his jaw, which could easily have been displaced. I wasn't sorry. Michelle and Trina, who were standing beside the dinner table, faking a conversation, came running toward us to see what had just happened. At this point, Victor was on the floor, and his nose started to bleed. Because of all the built-in emotions I had and constantly thinking of Brandon, it made me even angrier. In the midst of this turmoil, there was a silent storm brewing up inside Victor, and I had a feeling that he was going to retaliate. I kneeled down to him while he was still on the floor and kicked him in the stomach. He was quivering in pain due to the sharp force of pain that was aimed right toward his stomach. The room remained suspended in a heavy silence, broken only by the subdued sounds of Victor's labored breathing. This was no time for empathy; it was a moment of raw intensity and cathartic release in the face of overwhelming emotions.

I turned back to let the man breathe when I heard Victor say, "Oh, you will regret this."

Michelle came running toward the crime scene and freaked out. "Oh my god, Victor! Are you alright?" she screamed. "Alex, what the hell was that for? I am calling the police. This is completely not fair, and WHO DO YOU THINK YOU ARE?" she shouted.

Michelle was coming a little too close to me.

Trina, at the back, hollered, "Michelle, watch what you're saying. I am standing right here. Don't get too close."

"Or WHAT?" Michelle replied back while kneeling down and handing Victor a napkin. Afterward, she picked up the landline phone and called 911.

"You know why we came all the way here? It's because you have completely ruined our lives. We were nothing but amazing people to you both, Michelle. We know all about the dark magic you have done to us," Trina shouted from the top of her lungs.

"Yeah, and we also know that since the day we won the lottery, you all have been after our money. There were such evident signs before, although now it's too obvious. Just because you envy us, that doesn't mean that you ruin our life," I added.

Victor's gaze, unyielding despite the bruise covering the entire right side of his face, moved from Trina's face to mine. The lamp that was situated on the left of the living room reflected the despicable smirk that twisted his features. That sinister expression seemed to take over Victor's entire demeanor. His gaze lingered; the smirk was a silent declaration that, despite the evident physical toll, he harbored no remorse. He looked at Trina's face and then mine right after; there was still a despicable smirk on his face.

"Did you know? That because of your disgusting, filthy actions, it has also affected our son, Brandon, directly?" Trina added. "My baby boy is diagnosed with leukemia, and there's no way to reverse it right now," she cried.

As soon as Trina had informed them that, because of their actions, Brandon had been affected, they had no remorse. There was not even a second of hesitation or guilt that they might have felt toward him. None of them said anything. After seeing their reactions, it boiled my blood even more. Brandon, a baby boy who partially grew up in their arms and played with them, they had no worries about. He is my baby boy, and he is the one that is being affected the most by this. Their filth and hatred toward us were beyond my imagination, too. I was unable to grapple with the proper situation at first. I believe that if Trina and I had come here to confront them and make them realize their actions, they would be a little more remorseful. Although they clearly weren't. At that moment, I saw Michelle picking up the phone and calling the police.

Trina got a little worried because she knew that if the police were to get involved, they would easily make up a case against me. Her only worry was to get me out of the situation and leave. Although I had no intention of leaving just yet. I wanted to beat Victor up till he didn't at least say sorry. Not that it would change anything, although it would certainly make my trip a little better.

I had just turned my back around toward Trina because she had just warned me that Michelle was calling the police. Then, all of a sudden, I heard someone's shoes making a high-pitched noise as if someone was running toward me. Victor's shoes made that noise for a millisecond, and as soon as I turned around, Victor jumped and attacked me. He landed one of the heaviest punches I have ever encountered as a probation officer. As I could see him running toward me, Victor's towering frame and clenched fists loomed large, and his eyes were filled with hatred and intensity. The blood of the few punches I gave him was all dripped down to his linen shirt, making him look like a vampire. The punch caught me by surprise, almost like a thunderclap, temporarily deafening me for a split second. In the moment, the disorienting moment of silence, all external sounds faded away, leaving an echo of the punch ringing in my ears. I could see Trina from the right side of my eye, and she instantly clasped her mouth out of shock. I was able to tell that she did not like seeing me like this, especially because of my heart condition.

"Is that all you got, Alex? Come on, man, don't be shy," Victor said, while half of his face was already swelled and covered in blood. As soon as he said this, I was already even angrier and wanted to go in for another punch, not for the face this time but for the gut. As these words stroked the flames of my anger, a surge of determination fueled my next move. Channeling my inner John Cena, the air crackled with tension as the anticipation of the impending strike hung thick in the confrontations-charged atmosphere. I skipped toward Victor, and he was trying his best to slurry to the other side. Trina and Michelle were just standing on the sidelines, staring at what was about to happen next.

I took my left arm and threw another punch toward Victor, and with so much force, which enabled him to fall back on the couch. At that point, I believe that he became unconscious and was not responding. There was a moment of panic because Michelle had thought that something extremely critical had happened to Victor. The moment I arose from the couch to fix myself, I heard the police sirens from afar, which were slowly approaching Victor's home. I instantly knew that I was in a lot of shit.

There was no time to escape this mess.

Chapter Fourteen — Life is All About Lessons

Shortly after, the police arrived at Victor's place, and two patrol cars parked right outside Victor's doorstep. There were two patrol officers in each car, who immediately scurried into Victor's premises, gripping concealed firearms in their hands. Almost as if they were trying to catch thieves or persons in danger in this act. I'm not sure what Michelle told the police when she called them, although they all looked extremely pissed. The facial expressions that each officer had on their face were almost vain, ready to pounce and hunt down fresh meat. When they walked in, I was standing against Victor's fireplace, with my face red and bruised. I tried to hide my hands because they were a little bloody. My knuckles, especially since I threw some heavy punches on Victor. My knuckles were almost bleeding, too.

Victor was sitting on the floor, against the back end of a couch, to exaggerate his current position. His face was bleeding, and he had a sore black eye that bruised up so much that it felt like he was stung by a bee. His black eye turned purple, which led the police to believe that he was clearly the victim. Due to the punch I gave him in the stomach, his shirt was sort of disorientated, with muddy marks all over it. The police will definitely believe that I did beat him up and will arrest me.

Upon the prompt arrival of the police, an eerie suspense settled over the entire debacle, rendering everyone motionless. Nobody dared to move, and the officer's loud and stern voices definitely shook us all. We were all a little intimidated. It was by far one of those movie scenes that you watch on the TV. Michelle navigated the officer, saying, "Hi, Officer, we are being attacked. WE ARE BEING ATTACKED BY THESE TWO PSYCHOS!!!" Michelle started screaming from the top of her lungs.

"Ma'am, I need you to calm down. NOBODY move," one of the officers said. The other one had a gun positioned in his hands, pointed toward Victor and me.

"With all due respect, officer, no one is psycho here. Two old friends just got into a heated argument and began beating each other up," Trina added.

"TWO FRIENDS? TRINA? WHO ARE YOU KIDDING? We all know that you and Alex came here right at the beginning of my dinner party to ruin our night," Michelle argued. Her words, delivered with conviction, she spoke so ruthlessly, almost as if she wanted us to rot in jail. She left no room for doubt about the intensity of the situation.

"Ma'am, I need you to calm down. We are trying to do the best we can to solve this matter. Now, whose property is this?" The officer asked while looking directly at me. His intimidating glare scared me a little. The steely determination in his eyes instilled a sense of unease within me, telling me that I might get busted just now.

"It's my house. My name is Victor Andrews, and I am the rightful owner of this house," Victor squeaked.

"Alright, and who's this?" the officer asked while pointing at Michelle.

"She's my partner, soon-to-be wife, sir," he replied. The officer was jotting down notes at the back.

"And what is your relationship with these two individuals here?" the officer asked.

"I have no relationship with them. They barged into my house without my consent and beat me up, as you can see," Victor said while pointing at his face for proof.

Trina made a strange face after Victor's sly comments at the back.

"So if you have no relationship with them, how come you let them into your house? I can see that you have an alarm system and a gate to this private property. If they have no relation to you, then how come you let them enter?" the officer was insinuating.

"Uh, we were supposed to have dinner guests, as you can tell by the setup. So, we left the gate open for the guests. As far as having a relationship with them, we had a falling out a couple of months ago. They came unannounced," Victor said.

"Could you also add why we came?" I said.

"Quiet. We will come to you shortly," the officer said. "And what has this man done to you? Please elaborate and don't leave any information out since it could be useful to us," the officer asked Victor now.

"Well, as you can see, these two came over to our house, and the moment I got up to speak to Alex, he assaulted me. He threw a punch and then another punch over again. I tried to defend myself, and I flew in a couple of punches, too," Victor said under his breath.

"Is that it?" The officer asked.

"No, he also kicked me in the gut, and even ferociously, I think I need to head to the hospital officer."

"Alright. Now you, what is your full name?" the officer pointed toward me.

"My name is Alex Benjamin Robert, and that is my wife, Trina Joseph," I replied, I was very relaxed. The officer taking notes behind me stopped jotting down the notes and asked,

"Hey, are you the probation officer that was paroled in the station in the northeast for almost 15 years?" He asked.

"Yes, I am a former officer, although I have now retired and moved to Florida," I said.

"Oh! Well, good to see you, officer. I heard the station was distraught when you turned in your resignation letter. I hope you're doing well," he added.

"Well, *former officer*, you have seriously committed a crime now, and we have no choice but to take you down to the station. You have a right to stay silent. Anything you can say can and will be used against you in a court of law," the officer said.

"Oh my god, there is no need for that officer. You don't know these people. *They are evil*. My husband hasn't done anything wrong. These two have ruined our lives, and now my son has leukemia *BECAUSE OF THEM*," Trina shouted while tearing down.

"Relax, Trina, everything will be alright. Please call Aunt Mary's lawyer and tell him to meet me at the station," I hollered.

"Be quiet," the officer shouted.

"I'm coming with you. I don't want to stay here a second longer. And as for you, Victor and Michelle, karma will get back to you. What you have done to my family will come back right at you. Never forget this. God is watching, and God help you with what's coming to you very soon," Trina threatened.

They cuffed me, and I couldn't believe that this kind of day would also come to me. The first officer wasn't having any of this bullshit; he cuffed me so tightly and ruthlessly. I wasn't regretful for my actions one bit. Actually, I was proud. I couldn't sit on the sidelines while our entire lives were going to shit at this point. What I did with Victor was nothing compared to the harm and pain he had caused me and my family.

Trina and I left Victor's premises almost immediately while another officer stayed back to ask Victor and Michelle if they would like to press charges. As soon as I was leaving Victor's house, I could hear him saying, "Yes." I wasn't surprised. I knew that he would press charges to get some cash out of me. I didn't care; I had plenty.

As I sat in the patrol car, Trina was told to sit in the other car so that we didn't have contact with each other. We reached the station, and the first thing Trina asked me was, "Alex, what about Brandon?" We were supposed to leave in two hours. I completely forgot. We had to catch a flight to Florida in less than two hours, which meant that we were definitely missing it.

"Is there any way you can ask the nanny to look over him for two more days? I mean, Mark is just about to come and help me with this case," I asked.

"I suppose I can. Let me also call Papa," Trina said.

"No, don't call Papa. He will get so worried for no reason," I said.

"No, I have to, Alex; if there's any way I could fly him out to Florida, I will," Trina said.

"Okay," I said.

Trina went outside to inform Papa what had just happened, and while I was sitting there handcuffed, I laid eyes upon my best mate at the time, Michael, who was busy with a phone call. The second he put down the phone and looked out at the reception desk, he laid eyes upon me and suddenly started laughing.

"Alex!!! What are you doing here? And why are those handcuffs on you? You have got to be kidding me. What's all this about?" Michael was fascinated.

"Hahahahaha, man, I don't even know what to say. It's a long story. Could you please help me with a glass of water?" I asked.

"Yeah, of course, man! What a crazy time! I thought I would never see you like this. What a treat! Hahahahaha, how's everything? How's the family? Tell me everything," he asked.

He brought me a bottle of water and came and sat right beside me. "Hey man, what's the deal with this patrolling officer? He's really got a stick up his ass," I said.

"Yeah, man, he's in charge of the entire district. You know he takes his job really seriously. Now tell me, what's all this about?" he asked.

"Bro, I just beat the shit out of someone just now, and now he's decided to press charges. So they have brought me here. My lawyer is on the way, too. I hope I can get bailed out. I was supposed to leave for Florida in two hours."

"Geez. That man must have really needed it because I know your temper. You don't just explode until and unless someone really tests you," Michael said.

"Yeah, exactly."

Trina came back to the station and just informed me that Papa would take the next flight to Florida. He would be there with Brandon in less than 12 hours. I was so relieved because I was worried. Brandon had another doctor's appointment the next day, and he always needed someone for support.

In ten minutes, Aunt Mary's lawyer showed up and started haggling with the officers. They were being super rude to him because they knew that he was trying his best to get me off the hook. Although her lawyer was so top-notch, he knew his shit, and he knew how to navigate these police officers really well. They were arguing for about five minutes straight, and I could just tell that the man who arrested me didn't let me get off the hook so fast.

Aunt Mary's lawyer came back and informed us that since I admitted to physically assaulting Victor and they agreed to press charges, I would have to pay $35,000 for bail. He said that he had that covered since Aunt Mary left me with an abundance of cash that I still haven't touched. Although, he also said that he was trying his best to sue them right back since it was just a physical fight between two old friends. Nobody truly got injured during the fight, and these kinds of fights happen all the time. I informed him that Victor had made it very clear to the police that he didn't have any relationship with me, which made matters worse. In that case, I broke a couple of laws, and it might be hard to sue them back.

I told him to just pay the bail-out money so we could move on with our lives. The officer said that the bail would be issued the next morning and that I would need to stay in the lock-up for about 12 hours. To be very honest, I never genuinely thought this day would ever come. I was shocked that I, a retired probation officer, a man of this nation, would have to spend a night in the lock-up!!! What a crazy day!!!

I punched a man who very well deserved it, got arrested and spent almost $40,000 in just one go.

Talk about crazy things. I never knew that such a day would come, but now that it had, I felt pretty good about that. It was almost one in the morning, and I told Trina to go to the nearest hotel and stay there for the night. In the morning, as soon as I was bailed out, I could meet her there, and we could book our flight back to Florida. I also made sure that Trina took the medicine that Ma had given her because I wanted this evil magic to leave us for the rest of our lives.

While I was locked up in the jail cell, there were lots of emotions and thoughts that were rushing into my mind. There was so much that had happened to Trina and me in the last three years, and I was so grateful that we had fought that together. If I didn't have Trina by my side, I am not sure what I would've done to mend all this mess all alone. I am so thankful for the little family that we have created. It brings my heart so much joy and happiness that Trina prioritizes Brandon so much. I feel so loved by Trina and Brandon. I don't care about the rest of the world; if there's anything I've learned, it's that you cannot trust anyone in your life. Regardless of how amazing they seem at first, you cannot be too nice in this world; otherwise, people will walk all over you and take advantage of you.

If this bad patch in my life means anything, it is that, as long as you are faithful to your wife and prioritize your children, there is nothing else that you will need. Even before we won the lottery, Trina, Brandon, and I were so carefree and content in our lives that we didn't have to worry about anybody else. We were never in constant fear of somebody trying to harm us or somebody trying to get to us with bad intentions. We were blessed, and we are blessed to have each other. I am grateful to the lord that I haven't lost Trina in the process, despite their efforts to harm one of us directly; there is nothing else that matters to me other than my family being affected. And that gives me all the peace in the world.

Around 12 in the afternoon, another officer unlocked my cell and told me that my bail had been granted. I didn't want to sue Victor and Michelle, despite my heart telling me otherwise, because I knew that because of that, I would have to stay back home for a longer period. After being released from jail, I headed to the hotel Trina was staying at. I looked up flights to Florida so that we could get back home immediately. I couldn't wait to meet baby Brandon.

Once I headed toward the hotel, I realized that despite not harming Michelle and Victor the same way they had harmed me, I couldn't care less. I wanted to put all that negativity and dark phase of my life away. I just wanted to be surrounded by positive people and the closest people in my life — My family.

I met Trina at the Sheraton Grand Hotel, and when I went up to the room, I was in awe of how amazing and bespoke the rooms were. Trina was living in the executive suite with a stunning panoramic view of the city. The bathroom was uncanny; it opened up to the room, and it was all lavish. It was funny because I got to stay in a jail cell while Trina stayed at a five-star hotel. I booked the flight that took off at 11:05 pm, which meant that we would be home before Brandon woke up for school the next day. Papa was supposed to arrive in a couple of hours, which made me very happy. The only concern that was on top of my head now was Brandon's recovery; I wanted my baby boy to finally be healthy and live a normal life like any other kid is blessed with.

It was almost 6 am when we finally reached Florida, and I couldn't have felt better. Trina and I promised ourselves that we wouldn't speak about all that had happened now and just focus on Brandon. We made a pact that whatever happens in our life now, we will fight it together and not against each other. Our top priority was Brandon, and karma would surely get Victor, Fran, and Michelle.

When we arrived back home, around the walls that I felt the safest in, my heart was at ease. Papa was asleep, although once he heard us walk into the apartment, he hurried out in his robe.

"Oh my gosh!!! My children… How are both of you? Alex! My son! Is everything alright? Trina told me all that happened," he asked; he seemed so worried.

"Haha, Haha, Papa, you know my temper got the best of me. I couldn't help myself but to go and confront those freaks. That was the only thing that came to my head. And let me tell you that when I beat Victor up, there was no other feeling like that," I said light-heartedly.

"Hmm, I'm sure. You know, back in the days, I was no saint!" Papa laughed.

"Hey, hey, hey, not you two egging each other on now!" Trina laughed.

"So, I got in earlier, and I found Brandon with the nanny. I paid her, so she went home. I prepared Brandon some fresh food. Nutritious and healthy. Now tell me, Trina, when is his doctor's appointment? I want to go and see things myself," Papa asked.

"Oh, Papa, you didn't have to pay the nanny at all; I would've covered that. But thank you so much. Brandon's appointment is at 11 in the morning, so I would really appreciate it if you could take him since Alex and I are extremely tired?" Trina asked.

"Oh yes!! Of course, I will take that munchkin to the doctor's. You see, I want to have a word with the doctor myself. Also, I forgot to mention that Ma sent some medicines for Brandon and said that these would heal him perfectly fine. God willing, Brandon will be fine in no time," Papa said excitedly.

"They will affect him, right? I just want my baby boy to be fine already, and I am so worried. There is so much that is happening, and I can't do all this with the job and everything!" Trina panicked.

Papa walked over to her and gave her the tightest hug. Papa broke down into tears, hugging her daughter, and I could just tell that he was hurting so much. He began to cry hysterically, saying things like, "I pray to God every day to save you guys from this evil and throw it at me." He added, "I don't want you all to live in this constant fear. I want you to get out of this bad phase, I have lived my life, and I believe that I deserve all of this, not you guys!" He leaned in even more and hugged Trina tighter. I could feel all his emotions run down, and Papa seemed so vulnerable. His eyes, which were once filled with unwavering strength, now mirrored a depth of sensitivity that spoke volumes.

He felt as if the weight of the world was on his shoulders. His vulnerability radiated from him like an aura, inviting those around to witness a side of Papa that he rarely unveiled. I was so emotional at this point that I tore myself down. This memory that I will forever cherish will forever stay in my heart. You see, I never really understood the true concept of having a big family and the *only family-has-your-back* concept. I always thought that it was an over- exaggerated phrase that people always loved to throw at your face, although now I believe that I was wrong. Without Papa's help, his care, and his unwavering love for us, we would be lost. He is so selfless and truly prioritizes us like no other, and I am forever grateful for his support and guidance throughout life.

Papa had planned to visit Florida for only a week; he told Trina to book his flight back home for a week later. Although I urged him to stay with us. Since he had a 10-year-long visa, he actually moved in with us for a bit. He would be a great help to Brandon and also be satisfied with seeing Brandon's progress.

6 months later

After the relentless trips to the hospital and Ma's magical medicine, Brandon began to feel better. Thankfully, his chemotherapies and all his reports were coming out to be extremely great, with positive performance in each report. Brandon was finally able to balance the amount of cells that he was retrieving in his body. His white blood cells were gradually forming and functioning properly. It was definitely a slower process, although we finally made it. I couldn't be more grateful. Brandon is able to attend football practices at school, too.

After discussing life over and over again, Trina and I have made the decision to move once AGAIN! You are probably thinking we are a couple of nomads at this point in our lives, although I believe that this next move will be our final move. We have decided to move to Sacramento, California, and buy a massive house in the countryside. Since I am a retired old man, and Trina is getting old too, we just want to settle once and for all and unwind. We made this threshold of a decision because we wanted the next chapter of our lives without anyone knowing where we were. We want to be living our best lives while being secluded from the world. I remember looking at potential properties in Sacramento for a while, and one suddenly decided to pop up after searching for almost two months.

I wanted to invest in something that could be our forever home. Something where Trina and I could grow old in, a place that is cozy and away from all this hustle and bustle. Where we wouldn't have to worry about neighbors, the traffic, and the bipolar weather. Somewhere where we could live peacefully, happily, and content. We decided to send Brandon to boarding school in LA, which is not too far. We agreed that he could fly back on the weekends to visit us.

The home that I decided to invest in is situated in Sierra Oaks Vista, which is a prestigious gated community with unparalleled amenities and luscious green lawns. What sold me to this house was the grand foyer, which was adorned with intricate mahogany built-ins. Almost as if you were walking into a grand palace. Another great thing about this home was that it came with a large backyard. A backyard that extended to the green forests of California. Not to worry, though, because they had a safeguarding protection wall to segregate us from the mountain animals. Since we begged Papa to apply for United States citizenship, he decided to finally move in with us since the new house had an ample amount of room. We decided to give him a portion entirely for him, with a mini kitchen, a reading room, and a large bath. Trina was super excited about this move because of the weather and all the amazing pool parties she could throw for Brandon and his friends. We could have our famous family steak nights and celebrate the Super Bowl or Christmas.

***

As I end this heartfelt book, I am so glad to say that after this move, Trina and I have never felt safer or at peace. Moving to Sacramento, California, was the best decision, and I believe that we were destined to be here. Regardless of the battles we fought to get here, we are here, happier than ever and closer. Victor, Michelle, and Fran had no idea about this move, nor did any of us update our Facebook statuses to update our extended family or friends.

We decided to adopt some beautiful farm animals to take care of since it was a fun activity that I liked doing when I was younger. Papa and I would take the garden so seriously that every Sunday, we would garden our backyard. About a year after all these atrocities, I believe that Victor, Michelle, and Fran were still attempting to cast their evil magic on us, although they were out of our lives completely. Ma was continuously praying and fighting the dark magic back home in Vietnam, and we would send her monthly payments and extra money as a thank you. Therefore, I am forever grateful to that lady.

Our lives changed forever when Trina and I discovered about winning the lottery. I didn't expect our lives to change this drastically, and if someone had told me two years ago that I would be here through all the hardships and battles, I wouldn't believe them. The heart attack, Trina's deteriorating health, our constant fights, her miscarriage, and Brandon's health were all at stake. Although we overcame all of that, we are here — Content and happier than ever. All I have to say is that money is not everything. It's definitely a temporary push for your future, although happiness requires so much more. I still contemplate whether or not this lottery was a blessing or curse because there is so much that came along with it.

In order to attain happiness, you need to keep your family close, not be too naïve, but yet be kind in this world. Kindness comes to you unannounced and in so many unexpected ways. I believe that because I was so kind in this world, God helped me in the toughest times. My wife, my son, and my father-in- law are healthy and happy.

And nothing else in this world could give me more peace than that...